The Late Contessa

Dorothy Fletcher

CRIMSON
ROMANCE

F+W Media, Inc.

This edition published by
Crimson Romance
an imprint of F+W Media, Inc.
10151 Carver Road, Suite 200
Blue Ash, Ohio 45242
www.crimsonromance.com

ISBN 10: 1-4405-7200-3
ISBN 13: 978-1-4405-7200-5
eISBN 10: 1-4405-7199-6
eISBN 13: 978-1-4405-7199-2

Chapter One

I learned that I was an heiress on the thirtieth of April. It was Saturday, a true spring day, the sky baby blue with puffy white clouds, and the temperature in the high sixties. I could scarcely wait to get dressed and out of the house; the winter had been hard and long, and there was in the air that drifted through an open window in my brownstone apartment a kind of fragrance, like roses. It was, of course, simply the smell of new grass growing and the maple tree out front giving off the sap of renewed life.

It was my habit, on weekend mornings, to walk the dozen or so blocks to my parents' flat, for breakfast and a daughterly chat. Clad in casual pants and a shirt, I shrugged into a jacket and locked my door. It was only nine thirty, but the mail, in the East Seventies, was delivered early. I said hello to my next door neighbor, who was putting out her rubbish in a lacy blue nightgown, and ran down the stairs. I had a small package in my handbag…some cheese I had bought at a neighborhood shop, cheddar with pistachio nuts…it was a treat for my mother and father. I was in the best of moods: spring always does that to me, with its promise of summer ahead, the beach, coming vacation, sunny skies. I was humming as I put the key in my mailbox.

It was stuffed. There was a circular from a department store where I had a charge, a communication from my Congressman, and two letters. There was something else too, a stiff, bulky envelope which, when I eased it out, bore foreign stamps and the printed words VIA AERIA. I thought there must be some mistake, that what I held in my hands had been meant for someone else's box and had, inadvertently, been put into mine.

But there was no mistake. It was addressed to me, Miss Barbara Loomis, neatly typed on an electric. I fingered it and looked at the letterhead in the upper left hand corner. Whom did I know in Florence, Italy? I asked myself, but it was academic. I could see right away that this was not an ordinary letter but something quite different. For one thing, it was from a firm of lawyers, Predelli and Pineider, the Via Tornabuoni, Firenze, Italia, 50123.

Lawyers?

I was fascinated: I looked at the colorful stamps once more, turned the envelope over, felt its weight, and then tore the flap open. There was an impressive, legal brief inside, to which was attached a typewritten letter. The letter was addressed to me and, at the bottom, after the words, "sincerely yours," a signature, Antonio Predelli. And then I read the letter, after which I sat down on one of the stone steps leading to the street and read it again…and yet again.

At last I folded it, shoved it back into the crackly envelope, thrust it into my handbag and trotted over to the parental flat on East 81 Street, marveling…and wondering. Fred, the doorman, greeted me with some remark about the wonderful weather, told me I was looking perky and when I reached the eleventh floor and rang the bell, Millie let me in with a smile and her usual little peck on my cheek. There was the smell of coffee and bacon crisping. "I hope you brought your appetite with you," Millie said, as she always did, and in the big, cheerful living room my father was reading *The Times*, looking through his bifocals. He looked up and waved abstractedly, murmuring something. Mother was arranging flowers—tulips, fern, and baby's breath, in a crystal vase.

"Hello, there," she said.

I had to laugh. They were both so *scrupulous*…treating me like a friend instead of a daughter who, rather than take life easy in the ancestral co-op, with Millie to wait on me and launder my underthings, had apostasized and found an apartment of her own. Not a reproachful word had been said, but by their very absence of open censure there was an implicit animadversion. Or perhaps it was more basic than that. "It's your funeral, darling…"

However, I was content. I had one large, sunny room, with fourteen foot ceilings, an adequate if tiny kitchen and an adequate if tiny bath. With my decent-paying job at Plandome Press, Publishers, I could manage very well. They knew that, *pere* and *mere*, and respected me for it, but they would—and in subtle ways made it clear—have preferred their only child to remain at home until the finality of the marriage vows. I was not at all resentful, but rather tender and understanding. One day I too would know the wrench of parting from a child of my own, and there was no real generation gap in our little family. We coexisted.

I picked up a tulip and smelt it. It was a glorious scarlet, tight and unopened, with velvety petals. "Darling, don't bruise it," my mother said and I put a hand on her shoulder. "Listen," I said. "I've inherited some money."

"Oh?"

I suppose she thought I'd had a refund on my income taxes. She smiled and added, "Isn't that nice, dear?"

"No no, I mean it," I said breathlessly. "I'm rich. Someone's left me ten thousand dollars."

I had her full attention then. Holding a spray of baby's breath between her pretty and still young fingers she turned away from the vase. "What on earth are you talking about?" she demanded.

"It's true. Someone's left me money. Ten thousand dollars. What do you think of *that?*"

"Who?" she asked, squinting a little bit in disbelief. The way she'd looked at me as a child, telling some true but lurid story that had seemed to her a figment of my imagination. I remembered her questioning me. "Is that pretend, Barbara? Or real? Don't be afraid to say. I've a lively imagination myself."

I pulled the stiff envelope out of my handbag. "Here," I said. "Read it You'll see. It's true. I can't credit it, but there you are. I have a lot of money. She left it to me."

Mother took the envelope I handed to her. "But who?" she asked crisply. "Who is this someone?"

"Her name is…was…Mercedes. Mercedes d'Albiensi. She's…or rather was…a Contessa. Shen—"

My father threw down *The Times* and yanked off his bifocals. Mother dropped the sprig of baby's breath. Both said at the same time, *"Mercedes?"*

"You knew her?"

They stood together, after my father got up and went to Mother. They were fighting over the letter. "Let me read it," Mother said excitedly and my father, "But what does it *say*? What is this about money, about—"

"I can't tell until I *read* it," Mother cried. "Or else *you* read it, Howard, only for heaven's sake, how can anyone make head or tails of this unless…"

Then, like a good wife, she gave him the letter. He put on his bifocals again and read what I had read only a quarter of an hour ago. I remembered the approximate message.

> Dear Miss Loomis:
>
> Please read the attached, as relevant to your interests in the estate of the Contessa d'Albiensi, deceased. In order to clarify the meaning of the papers herein enclosed, which may be of little significance to you, may I say that the burden of this communication is to advise that you are an inheritor of the late Contessa Mercedes d'Albiensi, nee Reynolds, whose death occurred on the fifth of March of this year, 1971. The legator, the afore-mentioned Mercedes d'Albiensi was a great-aunt of yourself and has bequeathed this sum, free and clear, in your name —

And, a few sentences later, the amount of the inheritance. Ten thousand dollars. Bemused, I thought, who would have guessed, when I woke up this morning.

"But this is incredible," Mother said after a while. She and my father looked at each other. "Yes," he agreed. I said, "Then you knew her? This Mercedes?"

"Yes, of course. But—"

My father finished the sentence. "But after all these years!"

"All right, suppose we talk it out," I said, sitting down. "A great aunt, the man who wrote the letter says. On whose side?"

"Mine," Mother said.

"But we only knew her for a day or two," my father interrupted, looking stunned.

"Evidently she never forgot."

"I remember I liked her very much."

"So did I."

And then I heard the story, piecemeal, it's true, but at least the whole thing began to make sense to me. Mercedes Reynolds, who in fact had been christened Meredith (after the author) had, after leaving finishing school, taken the Grand Tour, ending up in Italy, where she had met and married an Italian gentleman of wealth and title, the Conte d'Albiensi, and never returned to the United States. Instead, she had changed the spelling of her name to Mercedes, had become enamored of her adopted country, had established a *salone* though bearing no children, and when the Conte died in the year 1949, had still not cared enough about the land of her birth to return. In short, the Contessa d'Albiensi, now dead, had become more Italian than the Italians...but had thought enough of at least one of her countrywomen to leave a sum of money to her.

Me, Barbara Loomis.

"Why?" I asked.

My parents looked at each other, and another chapter of the story emerged. Mother told it. "When your father and I went on our honeymoon, we stayed some of the time in Florence, and although we'd never met my Aunt Mercedes, we called her. Her villa is famous; everyone wanted to go there. I suppose I was showing off in front of your father. At any rate, we were invited, and spent a lovely two days at the Villa Paradiso. It was very beautiful, and we were so much in love. She took a fancy to us. Benevenute, her husband, a true nobleman and very handsome, liked us too. It was a memorable visit. Mercedes, in a spirit of what I thought was pure fun, said that if we named our first child Mercedes, she'd see that the child benefited. Well, of course we didn't name you Mercedes. But somehow she must have remembered. And only three years later her husband died. It was timing...I suppose... anyone could see that she adored the Conte...and there's so little family left, too. In the younger generation, just you, Barbara."

"I don't understand why I never heard this *interesting* story before," I said, annoyed.

"It was long ago," my father said, putting on his bifocals again. "You can't remember everything you know."

"*I* don't want to forget things," I said testily. "And now she's left me money, whereas, if I'd known about all that, I could have met her. It seems unfair to her. And to me, if you want my opinion."

"What's fair?" my mother asked, turning away. "It was our life, Barbara. It belonged to us, and it's our memory, don't forget that. There will be memories of your own, and *your* children will look daggers at *you*. But just the same, it will have belonged only to you. So try to understand."

"I'm sorry," I said penitently. "It's just that...well, having a total stranger leave me this kind of bequest...it touches me, makes me want to have known this lonely woman."

"I don't know why you say lonely," my mother objected, and I wondered if it wasn't a kind of guilt...all those years ago, on a joyous stretch of days, having been entertained by that woman, the Contessa d'Albiensi...and then forgetting.

"If she left money to someone she never even saw," I said, "she must have been lonely. Otherwise—"

My father crackled *The Times*, Mother fell to arranging flowers again. There was a quiet I tried to think of that woman's life, her husband dead, far from her own kith and kin, in Italy, on an estate run by servants, with the evenings leaving her lonely and sad. I couldn't help my resentment: I wanted to have known her.

"But then we all have our own lives to live," I said brightly, and mercilessly. "No time to spare for those less fortunate."

"My dear girl," Mother said, her eyes dancing with anger, "my aunt Mercedes left you a few dollars and cents. Don't you understand? She was worth a great deal of money. Ten thousand dollars? For a woman like that it's a token amount. I don't know why she did it, but I do know that it couldn't have left much of a dent in her capital."

She fingered baby's breath. "Don't bleed for her, silly girl. She had every creature comfort…and although your father and I live very well, we're dependent on the fortunes of this country and, if you don't realize it, the fortunes of this country, at the present moment, aren't too sound. We have many worries. Lonely? She could have adopted a child. She didn't need our child to leave money to. She could have—"

Unaccountably, there were tears in my mother's eyes. "Anyway, there was nothing I could have done," she said, under her breath. "She was only a distant relative."

"It's all right," I said uncomfortably. "I didn't mean to sound off. It's just that…she left me the money, and it touches me, haunts me."

"It haunts me too," Mother said, looking vacantly out the window. "It makes me remember when I was young. A bride. Today, all that seems so long ago. Nobody wants to get old. It was such a happy time for us. Italy, and the villa. But it was years and years ago. So long ago…those bright, sunlit days."

• • •

There were subsequent communications from Predella and Pineider. Apparently I wouldn't receive any monies until the estate was probated. Yet the circumstances had captivated me. And lying awake one night, I made some plans. My vacation was due in September, for I always liked to take it late, and I decided, with some high degree of excitement, that I would vacation in Italy. It didn't matter when I got my aunt's money; on my salary I could swing the air fare, and as for accommodations, I could put up at a pensione, for very little, and have my meals there.

I was determined to see the villa where my benefactress had lived a good many years of her life. And as soon as I had decided that, I fell asleep, peaceful and purposeful.

I applied for my passport the very next day. I had never been abroad. I would buy Italian grammers and Italian guidebooks. Not the Hamptons this summer, not Cape Cod. Florence, instead. And a look at the Villa Paradise, where had lived the woman, my great-aunt, whose largesse had made me richer by ten thousand dollars.

I just wished she were still alive. I wished I could have met this American woman who had turned her back on her homeland and chosen to live, far from her own kind, in Italy, where, I had been told, the sun shone *all* of the time, and where my own mother and father had spent many golden days in the beginning of their relationship…days so lovely, with their mutual feeling for each other, that my great-aunt Mercedes had never forgotten the looks they gave each other, and had, in memory of those adoring glances, made me one of her heirs.

Chapter Two

I arrived in Rome at eight o'clock in the morning, on the 19th of September. It was hot, *very* hot, in the crowded air terminal, but I was able to get a cab right away. I had booked into La Residenza, quite reasonable and anyway, it was only for overnight, since Florence was my destination. My room was not ready when I arrived at a little before nine, and I signed up for a city tour which took me to the Roman forum, St. Peter's, Hadrian's villa, and the Catacombs, and was back at the hotel just before the dinner hour. I dined across the street, at a ristorante called La Capriccio, and tumbled into bed at a little after ten. The Italian night, with its soft airs and sounds, was all around me, and I slept almost immediately.

Next morning I taxied, with my bags, to the Piazza della Repubblica, where I got my bus to Florence. There were some two dozen other passengers, mostly husbands and wives, and secretaries traveling together. I sat alone. I could have been in Florence in just under four hours, but this CIT tour had several historied stops and lunch in Perugia, which was why I had chosen it.

After a short stretch on a wide, modern autostrada, the bus left the main artery and wound through more scenic climes, entrancing country, verdant and colorful, fragrant, with flowers bursting out of the earth, stone houses and villas with siena-red, tiled roofs, tender valleys and purple hills. There were monasteries atop the hills, domed churches and cathedrals, campaniles cutting into the sky, ringing out the hours as the bus wound through the Tuscan landscape.

Spoleto, our first stop, was a charming, ancient little town that had become known for its annual music festival. We were given half an hour to stretch our legs, take snapshots and have coffee or a cold drink at one of the stands. There were postcards, of course, and venders selling trinkets, also some Italian children trying to get a few lira for hastily plucked field flowers that were already wilting in their sticky hands. I took a few snaps, bought one of the pathetic little bouquets and then heard a voice say at my shoulder, "Would you care for something? I'm thirsty, how about you?"

It was a youngish man I'd seen on the bus, traveling alone and sitting two rows ahead of mine. I had noticed him and I hadn't been the only one. He was tall and good-looking and I had seen a few of the young female passengers eyeing him. I was flattered that he had singled me out, and said I was thirsty too and would love a lemon soda. We stood sipping from straws, exclaiming about how good it tasted; tart, icy-cold, it was most refreshing. And then we were herded back into the bus again, to continue on our way.

When we reached Perugia and disembarked to head for the Ristorante Papagallo, there was suddenly a light hand on my elbow. "Could we have lunch together?" the young man who had bought me the lemon soda asked.

"Yes, of course. Thank you."

When we were seated on the rooftop restaurant, with its bright garlands of flowers all about and a sumptuous view of the valley below, he introduced himself. "I'm Peter Fox," he said. "From New York. Manhattan."

"I'm Barbara Loomis and I'm from Manhattan too."

He said he was staying in Florence for a few days; I said I was too. His hotel was The Grand, he told me and I said mine was The Continentale. We compared cameras, had a delicious lunch, made some small talk and were back in the bus again in an hour and a half. There was one more short stop, at Arezzo, before going on to Florence, where we arrived at a little before five o'clock.

One by one passengers were let off at their hotels; my friend Peter Fox, with a nod and a smile to me, left us at the Grand in the Piazza Ognissanti, quite a few people got out on the Lungarno

Acciaioli, in front of the Berchielli. I was the next to leave, along with two others. The Hotel Continentale was very pleasant looking, situated at the foot of the Ponte Vecchio. "I'm Barbara Loomis," I said to the man at the desk. "I reserved a single and bath."

He consulted his bookings. "Ah yes. Did you have a good trip from Rome?"

"A beautiful trip, thanks."

I surrendered my passport and was taken up to my room, *numero settantune.* It faced the Arno and the crowded approach to the Ponte Vecchio, and was very noisy, but I didn't care. It offered a stunning view, with church spires, golden domes and soaring campaniles across the river. I sat at the window smoking and having a little nip from the flask of scotch I'd brought with me, until the bright gold of the day changed to a misty violet, sentimentalizing. So here I was, old Barbs, in the cradle of the Renaissance. I could smell the antiquity, and by closing my eyes could imagine that it was the fourteenth century, that when I opened them again I would see Michelangelo walking along the embankment below, perhaps arm in arm with the young da Vinci.

Hunger pangs brought me back to the present. I leafed through my guidebook; one of the recommended restaurants was the Buca Lapi, in the Via del Trebbio. It was not a long walk: Florerice was a smallish city and I had been given a very good map by the hotel. I had a good dry martini on the rocks and was studying the menu when I happened to look up. One "happens to look up" because, I have always thought, of certain vibrations, and when my gaze traveled across the room I saw him, Peter Fox. He was not alone now, but with someone else, a middle-aged man, and the two of them were deep in conversation. They were at the other end of the room, but now and then I caught a phrase or two and it was not in English, but in Italian. I distinctly heard Peter say, *"Quanto dista da qui?"* To which the reply was, *"Sei chilometri."*

I mentally translated. Peter had asked, "How far is it?" and his companion had answered, "Six kilometers."

Languages come easily to me. Perhaps not German, but French, Italian and Spanish have overtones that strike my ear with a certain feeling of familiarity, and of course the Romance languages have much in common. If you knew Latin, it follows that the above tongues are not all that far afield. I listened, and after a while heard Peter say, *"Si, domani."*

Yes, tomorrow…

After that a large party of Americans came into the room, very voluble, and I couldn't hear anything else for their loud talk and laughter. While I was still feasting on my entree, a delicious steak Florentin, a local specialty, the two men, having already finished their meal, rose and left. For a moment, as Peter's eyes traveled incuriously around the room, I thought he had seen me, but obviously he had not. He threw down some lira for the waiter and soon vanished through the arched doorway.

I thought it rather a coincidence that we had chanced to take dinner at the same place and then tired, sated and ready for bed, I went back, through the charmingly lit Florentine streets, to my hotel. It took no effort to fall asleep; it had been a long day and, once in bed, pillowing my head on the downy mounds in their hand-embroidered cases, I was off in no time. It was only when the brilliant Florentine sun flooded the room that I opened my eyes. It was barely seven o'clock, but this was Italy, where the sun drenched the earliest hours. The blinding red of blood, dripping from a pierced heart, dazzled me from across the room; the framed picture of the throbbing heart of the crucified Christ, a little too realistic for my taste, stared at me. It was a Catholic country; they took their religion literally. It was somehow unsettling, and when my breakfast came up via room service, I turned my back to it so as to regain my appetite.

A pigeon whirred outside and, as I poured out my coffee, settled down onto the stone sill, cooing softly. And at nine o'clock, as the hands of my bedside clock turned, the hour bonged out from Giotto's belltower. It was one of the loveliest things about Italy, the bells eternally signaling the passing of time: it gave me an almost sensual pleasure.

I ate my breakfast with appetite. I was alone, without protection or any face I knew, but it didn't throw me; I felt, instead, a sense of high adventure. I was, in fact, feeling my oats and, making my preparations for the day, looked interestedly at myself in the mirror over the washstand, told myself I was a fairly striking-looking gal, and brushed my hair briskly. When I went down to the lobby, armed with lira-stuffed wallet, traveler's checks and camera, I greeted the desk clerk jauntily.

"*Buon giorno, come sta?*"

He smiled back, pleased. "*Buon giorno, signorina. Molto bene, grazie. E lei?*"

"*Molto bene.*"

"*Le piace stare qui?*"

"*Si, mi piace moltissima, grazie.*"

He laughed, appreciative of my efforts to commune with him in his language, and asked if I was bound for the Uffizzi. I said not today, that I had some business to attend to this morning, but that this afternoon I hoped to be able to go to the Villa Paradiso. "Do you know where it is?" I asked him.

"Oh yes. A very fine, old villa. Not far. About twenty minutes by car." He was curious. "You know someone there, signorina?"

"In a way. Could I ask you to make a telephone call for me?"

"Certainly."

I gave him the number of Predelli and Pineider and, after speaking to a receptionist, explaining who I was, I was switched to one of the lawyers.

It was Signore Predelli and, in moderately-accented English he said warmly, "Hello, how are you? Your letter reached us last week, saying that you would be in Florence and would like to stop in. By all means, signorina. We would be charmed. Where are you staying?"

"At the Continentale."

"We are very nearby. Our office is located, as you know, on the Via Tornabuoni, just across the street from Cook's. Take the lift up to the third floor; you will see our name on the door. Can I expect you this morning?"

"Thank you, I could be there in a short while."

"Wonderful. I will look forward to seeing you."

• • •

Signore Predelli was tall for an Italian, and solidly built, with a fleshy face. Rather sportily dressed, in a glen plaid suit and expensive necktie, with gold cufflinks gleaming as he held out a hand, he wore his thinning hair in violin strings in an attempt to hide the advancing baldness. He was natty, immaculate, and about fifty.

The fact that he was also fond of women showed in the dark eyes that looked me up and down, and as we walked back to his office there was a hand lightly on my arm. He offered me a chair and then sat down himself at a large, impressive desk.

"My partner, unfortunately, had to see some people outside the office," he told me. "But you can meet him another time. I am glad that *I* was not called out on business, for you are very pretty, and Italian men like pretty girls."

He leaned forward. "So you want to know about your aunt."

"Well, I'm naturally curious. I didn't even know of her existence until this happened. Apparently she lived most of her life in Italy."

"She was an interesting woman. Yes, Italy was her home, she became *very* Italian. A brilliant woman, a fine conversationalist. I miss her very much."

"Why do you suppose she left me money?"

"She probably was sorry not to have any children of her own. Sometimes, in these old families, the blood gets tired, used up. No strength for breeding. In this case it was like that. Who can say why? But it was so. But they were very happy together, so devoted. Well, signorina, there you were, in the country she left, a child of her family…and so she wanted to remember you in that way. And by the way, congratulations. I can imagine that you feel deeply grateful."

"I certainly do. And touched."

"Yes. You know she was a very rich woman. Very rich. It's nice, the amount you were left, and I am sure you will put it to good use. But she had a fortune and she left a fortune. We are still not sure of the exact amount, because some of her holdings are in the United States. But believe me, it is staggering. The villa is old and in some disrepair; however it is a good, solid structure and enduring. She lived a very frugal life these last years. A little bit eccentric, you understand? Clothing? She was not a fashion plate."

He smiled torerantly. "Well, she was *far* from a fashion plate. Food? She ate like a bird, except that when either my partner or I took her to Doney's. But on the other hand, when we were invited out there to the villa, I assure you that we came away hungry. She husbanded her money, as many old people do no matter how much there is of it. And so she left a huge nest egg for Elizabeth, who simply has no idea what to do with it. She doesn't even realize."

"Elizabeth?" I asked.

"Her companion of many years, Elizabeth Wadley, an Englishwoman. I believe they were girls together, when Mrs. Wadley lived for a few years in America…her father held some ambassadorial post. When they were both widowed, they met again and decided to make their home together. Mrs. Wadley was in a poor financial position, so it was a good arrangement for them. Poor Elizabeth, she must be heartbreakingly lonely."

"Did my aunt make any other bequests? Aside from me and this Mrs. Wadley?"

"Oh yes, of course…to people who worked for her, quite generous amounts. Otherwise Elizabeth Wadley inherits it all. But of course it is very nice, because when *she* dies, the estate, in toto, passes on to the former owners, the family."

"Who is the family?" I asked curiously. "The former owners you speak of?"

"By that I mean the Monteverdis. It's an old name, signorina, dating back to the earliest centuries. A great composer comes from that branch, Claudio Monteverdi, 1567 to 1643. His was the first great name in operatic history. Orfee, L'incoronazione di Poppea, Tancredi e Clorinda. The Monteverdis are very poor, but still they live very well on their estate, thanks to the Contessa."

"They live at the Villa Paradiso?"

A small smile crossed signore Predelli's face. He pushed ashes back and forth in a tray with a burnt-out match and at last confessed the reason for his mirth. "The Villa Paradiso," he repeated, still smiling. "Well, I don't think they like that name, you see. It was the Villa Monteverdi, but when the Contessa bought it she renamed it. And it is not a very imaginative name, you must agree. Even if she had called it the Villa Sciaccapensieri…which is like the French Sans Souci…it might not have offended quite so much. Perhaps she had read Feydeau—THE HOTEL PAPRADISO— and was thinking of that, though that has a comic connotation. At any rate, when the Monteverdis come into their own again, there will be a change of name for the villa. The old, rightful name."

He leaned forward. "But don't mistake me," he said. "They were enormously fond of your aunt. And she of them. There are two wings to the villa…in one of them the Monteverdis live. There is a stone wall at the back of the house, separating the gardens, but the gate of it is never closed. There was always privacy without familiarity."

He looked at me shrewdly. "You can't wait to see the villa, I'm sure."

"I'm very eager to see it."

He picked up a desk pad and wrote on it. "Here's the telephone number of your aunt. Mrs. Wadley will be most happy. And how to get there. It's only about six kilometers, not at all far out from the city. She'll certainly introduce you to the Monteverdis. You'll find them very simpatico. The Principe and Principessa will not be called by their titles. Simply address them as signore and signora."

"You mean they're—"

"It doesn't mean anything any more. It's considered vulgar, except in jet set circles, to use titles as a form of address. You see, signorina, in Italy it is the same as anywhere else. The best people don't—"

He smiled again. "We have a saying. *La genie semplice e la migliore. Quella che si da le arie ci fa ridere…*"

"I know some Italian," I said. "But I can't translate *that*."

"Roughly," he said, "it means 'people of quality don't put on airs'."

" *'Ridere'* means to laugh, doesn't it?"

"Ah hah! You *do* know some Italian! All right, what I said was this, and it is a good thing to remember. 'Simple people are the best…they laugh at those who put on airs.' You don't want to be laughed at, signorina? No, of course not. Address them as signore and signora. They will respect you for it."

Chapter Three

I called the Villa Paradiso after I left the attorney's office. The desk clerk obliged again, but there was such a long wait before the ringing stopped that I was sure my aunt's companion was not at home. But at last a brisk, very British voice said, "Hello, hello."

"Mrs. Wadley?"

"Speaking."

I introduced myself. "I'm Barbara Loomis, the Contessa d'Albiensi was my great-aunt. She left me an inheritance. I'm here in Florence, and of course I'd like to see the villa, Mrs. Wadley… and meet you."

"I beg your pardon?" There was a loud throat-clearing. "Who'd you say this was?"

"It's Barbara Loomis," I repeated patiently, enunciating clearly. She was well on in years, was perhaps hard of hearing. "Mercedes d'Albiensi was an aunt of mine. She left me some money in her will. I'm here, in Italy. In Florence. Would it be possible for me to pay you a visit, Mrs. Wadley?"

"Why, my word!" There was a booming laugh. "This is little Barbara? You mean—"

"This is little Barbara," I agreed. "Except that I'm not so little. I'm twenty-four."

"You don't say!"

I started all over again. "I'm here in Florence. I'd love to see the villa. I wondered about this afternoon."

"*Indeed* this afternoon. What a delightful surprise. Hello, my dear. Yes, do come out. I shall be at home all the afternoon and evening. You'll have dinner with me."

"Oh, thank you, but I wouldn't dream of—"

"Oh, but you must. It will be like old times, to sit at table with someone else. I won't take no for an answer."

"It's extraordinarily kind of you, Mrs. Wadley. But you must tell me what to bring. A little steak? Lamb chops? I can get something at the markets here."

"Oh, I have provisions," she said largely. "Don't fret yourself. What time will you be here, dear?"

"I thought about—"

"Then shall we say at around six?" she said, interrupting me. "Good, I'll see you then. How jolly! It will be *such* a diversion for me. We shall have a splendid time. There's a television. The reception's poor, but no matter. There's a hair dryer too; you'll like that. Young people are so fond of washing their hair every two or three days. So then I shall see you about sixish."

"Well, fine," I said, a little dazed at mention of TV and a hair dryer. "But please tell me what to bring. I could pick up some meat...or fish..."

"I have everything like that," she insisted and then, in a rush, avidly, "You might get some cheese sticks and those lovely salted almonds. And the vol au vents. I do so like them. On the Via Parione, the British shop. It's not hard to find; it has the crest of the Empire on the glass door."

There was a kind of buzzing, as if she had faded away, and then she said, "Sorry, I dropped the phone, are you there?"

"Yes, I'm here."

"Good-bye, then. The taxi will be about four hundred lira, with another hundred for a tip. Don't give him more than that, no matter how threatening he becomes. They see a foreigner coming, but don't let him bully you. *Capisco?*"

"*Capisco,*" I said, but she had already rung off.

• • •

I found the British shop Mrs. Wadley had mentioned, and she was right…their wares were mouth-watering. I bought the vol au vents and the cheese croutons and a pound of "those lovely salted almonds," and went in search of a taxi. There was a stand in the Piazza di Trinita nearby; I had only a few minutes' wait. Inside, I told the driver the Villa Paradiso. He knew instantly, gave me a respectful and rather inquisitive look in the rear view mirror and pulled away with a snarl of wild rev of the motor.

We went through narrow streets, passed through an austere Roman gate and the remains of an ancient city wall, and then started to climb. The road was steep, as narrow as a needle, and serpentine. At every dangerous curve my driver leaned on his horn, but he was going at a fast clip and driving, essentially, blind…you had no way of knowing what was just round the bend. I found my fingers whitening as they clung to the leather of the seat; finally, I said, *"Per favore, troppo veloce…lentamente, per piacere…"*

"Si," he said indifferently, and slowed up not a whit. It was horrendous…at any moment I expected a collision…the scream and wrench of metal against metal. But nothing of the sort happened, though when the cab finally screeched to a stop, I was shaking as with the ague.

"Quanto costa?" I asked, taking out my wallet.

He looked at me, in the mirror over the dashboard, consideringly. Then said, "One thousand lira, signorina."

"No," I answered, my chin out. "The people here told me it would be four hundred. Here's five hundred. I won't be cheated, particularly after that awful, frightening ride. *Capisco?"*

There was no argument. He took the five hundred lira, smiled pleasantly, wished me a fine evening and, jerking a thumb in the direction of the villa at our right, said, *"Bellissima,* that. Old, old. The family Monteverdi. Good people, a good name, old, old."

He backed up, gunned his motor, and was off in a cloud of dust. I stood in the roadway, watching him disappear into the distance. It was just a little before six o'clock and would not be dark for another two hours, but just the same there was the violet foreshadowing of the evening slowly coming on. The earth smells were everywhere, warm and beautiful and primal…and the aroma of a thousand flowers enriched the dying day. The sun still scorched, but a vagrant breeze had sprung up, whispering the leaves in the trees. There was the busy twittering of bird life, and a cuckoo sang its song. A cow lowed, in the distance, wanting to be milked, and six solemn notes bonged from some nearby belltower.

The villa, rambling, large, of rough stone almost entirely smothered in climbing vines, was behind a brick wall whose rusty iron gate hung open and beyond which there was a courtyard, very medieval-looking. I could picture horses stabled there, with grooms currying them, but in today's time it was a garden, wild and untended, but pretty and rustic. I could see at once, that, architecturally speaking, the beauty of the villa would be at the back of the house where, I knew, there would be a splendid view of the valley.

I went through the courtyard and then, after climbing a half dozen worn steps, clanged the heavy door knocker. I waited, but nothing happened. I reached for the knocker again, gave it three smart raps.

There was still no answer.

She did say six o'clock, I explained to myself. Didn't she?

I rapped once again.

Nothing.

Well, this was a strange welcome, I thought and, making up my mind, went through the courtyard again. This time I plodded along a gravelled pathway that led to the back of the house, passing a small blue Lancia parked to one side. My footsteps crunched on the tiny pebbles. I was a little uneasy. Supposing there had been some error on my part…or some misunderstanding on hers. There was no way I could get a taxi back to town. I was annoyed too…after all…

And then I came to a most beautiful place. I was at the back of the house now, and standing in a garden that was so wonderful I had to draw in my breath. I had been right about the view. I was looking down on the glory of Florence. There was the Domo, the octagonal Baptistry, and the exquisite belltower of Giotto's creation. Lacy churches dotted the landscape, the medieval campanile of the Palazzo Vecchio loomed; the Arno spun its way, with its many bridges, like a silver thread, below the lovely, lovely embankment.

I gazed, exalted. I felt as if I could reach out and scoop that miniature city, far below, into my hands, hold it there, captured, like a fistful of jewels.

It was at that moment that I heard the sound. For a minute or two I couldn't pinpoint what it was…a light, sighing, quivering breath of sound…

Like someone crying.

Why, it *was* someone crying, I thought, and a fragment of memory flitted through my mind. When my little sister had died of meningitis…behind the closed door of my parents' bedroom, the muted sobbing, like the tearing of silk…smothered behind a despairing hand.

I peered through sheltering trees and then I saw the figure kneeling on the ground. Like a penitent, with head bowed, and the dry sobs, almost but not quite soundless, coming from that crouched figure. I walked quickly toward it, and stood at last beside an old woman whose faded blue eyes were diffused with tears. White-haired, thin as a rail, with a long, sinewy neck, nose strong and carved and her mouth a red gash in the parchment white of her aging skin, she was bent over some object on the ground.

"Mrs. Wadley?" I said.

She looked slowly up at me, and her eyes were filled, not only with tears, but with shock and horror. Then I looked down, past her. The woman's hands were threaded through a coat of fur. The coat belonged to a dog. A dead dog. I had never seen a dead dog, but I knew there was no life left in that little animal. Its eyes were open but unseeing. There was a foam of blood on its muzzle. It was rigid.

And then the woman spoke.

"He's dead too," she said. "And now Paolo's dead too."

"I'm so terribly sorry," I said, and knelt beside her. "Was he very old?"

"Not old enough to die."

"But—"

She repeated it. "Not old enough to die. Oh, I know. Don't think I don't know. It's a warning, you see."

I stared at her. "A warning?"

She laughed, a strange laugh, looked down at the inert body of the little animal. She stroked its fur once more and then gathered the small body into her arms.

"He's still warm," she said softly. "He didn't want to die. He grieved, yes, when she left us. But there was me, and he knew I needed him. He wouldn't have wanted me to be alone. Oh, it was deliberate. They're trying to frighten me."

She struggled up. I helped her. "Oh yes," she said, as she regained her feet. "Yes, I know. Everything's very clear."

And then a change came over her. Her face grew wary. There was a long silence and then, "Oh, you're little Barbara."

"I'm Barbara Loomis. You're Mrs. Wadley?"

"Yes, how are you, my dear?"

It was grotesque; with the dead animal under one arm she held out a hand, shifting the weight of the dog. "Welcome to the Villa," she said. "Come inside, do. I'll give you some Punt a Mes, then I must have Gianni see to Paolo's burial. He will be desolate, you know. He so loved our little boy. I want him buried under the twisted pine."

She pointed. "That one. It was his favorite resting place. Now it will be his eternal resting place."

"You mustn't worry about me," I protested. "I'll wait here. Please don't—"

"No no," she insisted. "You'll have an aperitif, and I shall be back as soon as I can." She cradeled the moribund dog in both arms and led me across the lawn to two lovely french doors that stood open. She stood aside for me to enter, and there was a forlorn drop on the end of her nose. She sniffled it away and pointed to a stand with liqueur bottles. "Help yourself, please, dear. If you don't, I shall be most unhappy. I shall be back directly. Just let me attend to this sad undertaking. I'll try not to be too long."

"Please don't hurry. Are you sure I can't help?"

"Thank you, but Gianni and I will do it together."

And then she left me, carrying out the dead animal like a sacrificial offering. I was, to say the least, shocked and put off by the whole thing. I thought it would be a long time before I forgot about those dead, glassy eyes, that blood-specked muzzle.

And the incoherent spate of words. "They're trying to frighten me…it's a warning…"

I poured out some liqueur into a small glass, lit a cigarette and looked about. It was a vast, white-walled room with a vaulted ceiling, like that of a cathedral, lancet windows, and an enormous open hearth. In the center of the huge room a gigantic trestle table, with the golden patina of age, was piled with books, ceramic pieces, pewter trays and a great earthenware bowl large enough to hold Ali Baba or one of his forty thieves. It was filled with masses of dried flowers. There was a big concert grand at the farther end of the room, its top down and over it an old-fashioned, fringed and flowered shawl. And on top of the silk shawl, an abundance of gilt-framed photographs.

I got up and went over to look at the photographs. Right away I saw Mrs. Wadley, in beach attire (very modest), in front of a striped cabana. Perhaps on the Lido in Venice, I thought…or Ischia, or Capri. Several gentlemen of various shapes and sizes and ages smiled at me, one of them with an impressive black mustache curled up at the corners like Toscanini's. There were two pretty children in pinafores, with their pretty mother. And—I nearly fainted with surprise—a snapshot of two people who were my mother and father of years ago. There was the same snap in an album back home. It was so odd to see it there among a raft of strangers, two people the late Contessa had known twenty-five years ago, for a day or two, and whom she had never totally forgotten.

Truly, the ways of the human heart were inscrutable.

And then, as I put the framed snapshot back on the silken scarf, I saw my dead great-aunt. That it was she took no conjecture on my part. It was signed, at the bottom, in a bold, round hand. "To Elizabeth, with love," it read, and the woman in the photograph was handsome and, yes, regal, with a crown of iron-gray, strong hair that haloed her fine face. She looked a little bit like the Tsarina, with that kind of chiselled nose, and the clear blue eyes.

She must have been a beauty in her youth, I thought, and then saw her in her youth. It was unmistakably the same woman, twenty or thirty years earlier, in the clothes of the period, standing arm in arm with a dark-eyed man who was not quite as tall as herself, and rather frail-looking. His head, which was handsome and finely-shaped, seemed a bit too large for his small frame. He was looking straight into the camera, but Mercedes was turned sideways, gazing worshipfully at him.

I had just put the photograph back when I heard someone coming into the room. I was primed to see Mrs. Wadley, but it was not she. It was a man, tall, slim, dark, young…and looking curiously at me. We eyed each other for a second and then he said, in English but with a charming accent, "Hello, I'm Giovanni Monteverdi."

I said I was Barbara Loomis, and mentioned the dog. "Yes," he said. "It's terrible. He must have gotten into some weed-killer."

"I feel in the way," I explained. "I'm wondering if I shouldn't call a taxi."

"No no, don't leave her. It will be a bad evening for her. She will be with you soon, just make yourself comfortable, signorina."

He excused himself. "I need a spade, and some kind of box, so that we can lay Paolo to rest in the earth."

He went away and in a few minutes I saw him walking round the back, carrying tools and a cardboard box, walking springily on the balls of his feet. He carried himself well. I hadn't failed to notice the length of his eyelashes.

And then he vanished out of sight.

It was almost half an hour later when Mrs. Wadley returned through the french doors. Pale and drawn, she apologized for keeping me waiting so long. She had regained her composure and, in spite of her pallor, smiled pleasantly and said how happy she was to meet me. "You're so good-looking and have such beautiful legs," she told me. "American girls have such a *style*."

She pulled off a pair of garden gloves, white cotton and stained with the brown of the earth, so that I knew she must have helped Giovanni make the "final resting place" for the dog, Paolo. She saw that I had helped myself to the liqueur, nodded approvingly, and filled a glass for herself. We sat together on a rather worn sofa, and, lifting her glass, she said, *"Buona fortuna."*

Then, her eyes keen and sharp as she gave me a piercing look, she said quietly, "You must excuse, please, my earlier hysteria. I don't know what I said in my excitement…and sorrow…but I was, of course, shocked and—"

She twisted her hands together. I saw the knuckles go white. But it was with a calm and clear voice that she went on. "When one is under stress," she said, "one says ridiculous things."

For a moment she was silent. Except for the whitened knuckles, there was no sign of agitation. "Well," she said, at last, "let's forget it, shall we? You've met him, Gianni. He said so. I like him, that nice boy. I like Italians, don't you? I've spent a good many years of my life living with them. You must meet Gianni's family. His father and mother. And the other son, Benedette, whose wife is Francesca. They have a beautiful little girl, Eleanora. But you must be hungry! It's almost seven o'clock."

She picked up her glass again and drained it, then saw the package I'd brought, exclaimed over it. "I'll just put them on a tray," she said. "Thank you, my dear. Aren't they beautiful? I'll be right back. And then I'll make us a lovely dinner. You must be starved."

She refused all offers to help, and when she left me to prepare dinner, I went to the piano. It was somewhat out of tune and the keyboard was a little stiff, but I played a few Chopin preludes and was beginning to feel quite at home by the time Mrs. Wadley wheeled in a loaded cart. The smells were wonderful. "It was so nice to hear the music," she said, as she wheeled the cart over to the windows, where there was a small table with a centerpiece of flowers in a pewter vase. She didn't lay a tablecloth, but put the dishes right on the well-worn wooden table. Then she drew up two chairs, cane-bottomed.

I said it looked marvelous, and she beamed, uncorking a bottle of wine with great professionalism. She filled two smashingly lovely crystal goblets and then sat down opposite me.

"*A tavola nonsi invecchio,*" she said, ladling food onto my plate.

"That means—"

"At the table one doesn't grow older."

I looked at the wealth of food and remembered signore Predelli's comment about the paucity of vittles served by the two women. Well, times had changed, I thought wryly. There was enough food for four people; furthermore, Mrs. Wadley ate voraciously. As if she had been starved for a long time. But then, of course, when Mercedes was alive, it had been the Contessa's house, the Contessa's way of doing things. Perhaps, like the signores Predelli and Pineider, Mrs. Wadley had habitually left the dinner table unappeased.

I was trying to form a picture of my great-aunt in my mind. More than that, I was determined to find out everything I could about her. It was a kind of challenge, a compulsion to *know* her, to ask, discreetly, questions that would give me a clue as to Mercedes'ss life-style and character. After all she had left me a tidy sum of money. But it was more than that...it was like wanting to walk into a picture on the wall, to enter into the mind of the man who had painted it.

And so, when Mrs. Wadley casually said that of course I would have dear Mercedes's room, where I would be quite comfortable, and the use of the car whenever I wanted it, I didn't protest for very long. I said I had booked a room at the Hotel Continentale and wouldn't dream of imposing on her, but she insisted so vehemently that I stay at the Villa Paradiso (and in fact it was exactly what I wanted) that in the end I gave way gracefully, thanked her profusely and when I left, after my hostess called me a taxi, I said I would be round, bag and baggage, before siesta on the following day.

She said one last thing before I left, a thing that remained in my mind as I drove the perilous trip back to the center of town, at the same reckless rate of speed as the earlier trip out (only it was far more intimidating in the darkness). Framed in the dim light of a lantern as she stood in the doorway, she said, "You've no idea."

Her brisk, clipped British voice was emphatic, and she was smiling in a kind of triumphant way. "Of course you've no idea. But I shall sleep so much better tonight. Knowing I won't be alone. It's so *good* of you."

That was all; her voice trailed off, and I climbed into the cab, waving through the window. She stood there watching me go, and as the taxi gained the roadway, she was a little like a ghost, or a wraith, a tall woman standing there in the nimbus of the lantern. And then we plunged into the night, on that horrible, narrow road, with me bracing myself. But we passed only one car on the way down. Both cars came to a full stop, almost nose to nose, and then with both drivers muttering imprecations, they eased past each other without even grazing fenders. At the hotel I didn't even ask how much the fare was, but gave him a five hundred lira note. He complained bitterly.

"Not enough."

"It's what I paid going out."

"But it's night now."

"Is the gasoline more expensive at night?"

He sighed, giving me a sidewise look of, perhaps, grudging admiration for my perspicacity. I told myself I was learning fast and, after setting my alarm and lighting a cigarette, pulled out the postcards I had bought. But then I pushed them aside. They could wait. I would have plenty of time to write postcards at the Villa Paradiso.

Chapter Four

I was up early again the next morning, too early for room service, so I dressed, locked my bags and went downstairs to tell the concierge that I was checking out. "Oh, but I am so sorry, signorina," he said. "You're leaving Florence already?"

"No, I've been invited to stay at the Villa Paradiso."

He clucked, looking impressed, and totaled up my bill on the adding machine. I paid it, said I was going to take a short walk, and would he order me a taxi for eleven o'clock. Then I went outside, strolled over the The Ponte Vecchio, and then back again to the Lungarno Acciaioli, where there were several outdoor cafes. I sat down at one of them, ordered breakfast and then, leaning back, saw a familiar face.

It was that of the man who had sat opposite my traveling companion, Peter Fox, at the Buca Lapi the night before last. He was reading an Italian newspaper and a cigarette dangled from his lips. There was a cup of espresso on the table in front of him.

I was buttering my roll, watching him, when I saw him lift a hand in greeting. He took the cigarette out of his mouth, crushed it out in one of the yellow ricard ashtrays and pulled out a chair next to him.

"*Buon giorno,*" he said, and another man threaded his way past the tables, returning the greeting.

The newcomer was the lawyer I'd met, Signore Predelli.

He saw me almost at once, stood up immediately and, murmuring something to the other man, came over to my table.

"*Buon giorno,*" he said cordially. 'Oh yes, you are staying at the Contientale which, like my office, is just a step away. I almost always have my second breakfast at this cafe. Well, are you enjoying your stay, signorina?"

I said yes indeed, and then went on to explain that I was moving out of the Continentale into the Villa Paradiso. An odd expression came over his face, almost one of disapproval, and then he smiled pleasantly again. "How delightful for you," he said. "But come, you must meet my partner, Pineider. I'll have the boy bring over your plate."

He signalled a waiter and then led me over to the other table. "This is the Contessa's niece," he said to the other man, who had risen, a napkin in one hand. "And Miss Loomis, this is my partner, Arturo. Signore Pineider. Imagine it," he said, when my breakfast dishes were brought over and we were all seated, "the lovely young signorina is to stay at the villa."

"No!" Signore Pineider cried.

"Yes, I'm going there in a short while. Isn't it intriguing?"

"So you got on well together, you and Mrs. Wadley," Signore Predelli said.

"Famously. I was invited there last evening. To be sure, it got off to a bad start. My aunt's dog died. I kept knocking, but there was no answer. Then I went round to the back and there was Mrs. Wadley, bending over the dog. Gianni said he'd gotten into weed-killer. It was quite a shock. I could see she didn't want to be alone, and accepted her invitation to stay at the villa."

"The dog?" Signore Predelli repeated, sharply. "Paolo?"

"Yes, it was upsetting."

I was conscious of a long look exchanged between the two men. I finished up my rolls and jam, felt the sun flaming across my face, thanked Signore Pineider for refilling my coffee cup from the silver urn and said yes, I knew I was going to like Italy. But there was something in the air, something I couldn't fathom. Both men, though they were talking easily, being flatteringly attentive, had a kind of reserve about them. If there was something wrong about my staying at the villa, why didn't they say so? And then, looking at Signore Pineider, I thought of him at the Buca Lapi, sitting next to the American, Peter Fox.

It had been a surprise to find myself in the same restaurant as Peter, but the fact of him being with one of my aunt's lawyers was carrying coincidence a little too far. I remembered Signore Predelli saying, "… many of the late Contessa's holdings were in America…"

There must certainly be some connection between Peter Fox and the lawyers Predelli and Pineider…something, it seemed more than likely, related to Aunt Mercedes. Well, what of it?

Yet I felt uncomfortable, somehow. As if there were something that was being kept from me. I looked at Signore Pineider, the cigarette dangling again from his lips. The sun made a blinding haze that gave everything an eerie shimmer. I put down my coffee cup.

"I must go," I said. "I've ordered a taxi, you see."

Both men stood up. Each kissed the back of my hand. *"Arrivederci"* Signore Predelli said genially.

"You must call us," Signore Pineider said. "We'll dine at Doney's some evening soon. It was a great pleasure to meet you, signorina."

I felt their eyes following me as I walked along the Lungarno back to my hotel. I knew they were watching me walk away. Again I thought, there's something in the air.

• • •

I was at the Villa Paradiso at twenty after eleven. The driver lifted my bags out and took them to the door. This time I paid a thousand lira, owing to the weight of the bags. I was just about to lift the heavy knocker when I heard a soft voice. Turning, I saw a little girl, eight or ten, so exquisite that I thought of the young Infanta of Spain as painted by Velasquez. She had the tawny hair of Tuscany, and her cheeks were like strawberries. Over one arm was a wicker basket and her eyes were like sherry, enormous and limpid.

"*Buon giorno,*" she said.

I was just about to answer when Giovanni Monteverdi—or Gianni, as Mrs. Wadley called him—came through the courtyard. He saw me and waved. "*Buon giorno*, hello," he said.

"Hello, Gianni. Will you introduce me to the young lady?"

"Sure," he said and, bending, snatched a kiss from the peach-bloom cheek of the little girl. Teasing, he reached for the basket over her arm.

"No no," she cried, taking it away from him.

"Secrets, secrets," he said, shaking his head. "Speak the English, little one. This is an American young lady. Tell her you are happy to meet her. *Si?* Now, darling, you say."

The beautiful child looked up at me, dimpling. "How do you do?" she said, and Gianni laughed. He walked up to me, holding the child's hand. "Miss Barbara, this is my little niece, Eleanora. Eleanora, this is an American young lady, say hello nicely."

"Hello, signorina."

"Hello, Eleanora."

"These are your bags?" Gianni asked. "Okay, I'll take them in for you. Later, though. Now you must meet my family. They are in the garden."

"Well, I—"

"Ah, come on," he said, in a friendly way, and I thought why not, I was not averse to meeting a prince and princess, even if I had to remember to address them as signore and signora. "My father has a headache," the little girl said to me. "Nonna makes him tea. Papa didn't sleep well last night. Poor Papa."

"My brother Benedetto has a headache very often," Gianni said, smiling. "He drinks too much, that one." There was a teasing glint in his eyes. "Now, don't say I mentioned it, but he gambles too much also. Loses…and then gets a headache."

"I won't say a thing," I promised, smiling back.

"It's different with me," he boasted. "I don't need the tables… or the *vino.* I see a lovely face, it makes me feel good, so I don't need anything else. And then I have good friends."

He put his arm on the little girl's shoulder, as we walked round the side of the villa. "This young lady is one of them. Oh, sometimes we fight and hit each other, but—"

"That's not true, Gianni!"

"Come on, sometimes you're a very bad girl."

"No!"

And then we reached the Monteverdi's garden. I felt as if I were in a scene by Pisarro or Seurat. Seated around a large white garden table that was sheltered by a flowered umbrella sunk deep in the earth, the family was gathered. A man and woman, elderly, she with springy white hair gathered into a bun at the nape of the neck and he with beetling brows and piercing eyes, nose like a hawk.

There was also a younger man, mid-thirties, stocky, no longer really handsome but bearing the traces of a once good physique. He had a newspaper open on his lap. A pretty, rather plump woman with her hair caught up in a tulle net at the top, pearl earrings and dressed in a peignoir, was lighting a cigarette. The sun gilded everything.

"Papa, Mama," Gianni said, and led me forward.

There are certain moments you know, even at the time, that you will never forget. It was this feeling I had as I stood there in the late morning, meeting the Monteverdis for the first time. The bright ambiance of the Florentine day, the flowered daisies of the umbrella thrust through an opening in the garden table, the quivering of the leaves in the trees, the picturesque little girl with the basket over her arm, the young couple sizing me up—she with bright, curious eyes and he with the appreciative glance of a man who liked nice-looking women—the proud and acquiline faces of the older couple, the Principe and Principessa…it was as if time suddenly stood still, so that I could store the recollection in my brain.

And the incredible beauty of the city that lay at our very feet, with the clam-white houses and pinkish domes and the gleaming crosses and gray-blue of the river, meandering…it framed itself in my mind, and I knew that when it came time for me to leave this place I would weep for the lost beauty of it, ache for it, as for a lost lover.

"This is the Contessa's niece," Gianni said. "Miss Barbara Loomis." He turned to me. "My mother and father. My brother and his wife. Welcome to the villa, signorina."

"Hello," I said. "*Buon giorno.* I'm so very happy to meet you all."

Gianni's brother pushed back his chair and stood up. The older man made a show of rising, in deference to the stranger, and then leaned back in his chair again, saying, "Welcome," in a voice like a singing bass. His son reached for my hand, kissed the back of it and said, "My wife, Francesca."

The pretty lady smiled ravishingly. "Hello, darling," she said.

The Principessa was graciousness itself. "We are happy and proud to meet you. Please sit down. No, not there…the sun will be in your eyes. Here, in the shade. Would you like coffee or tea?"

"Coffee, please, thank you."

She picked up the silver urn. "Gianni, sit down. Don't stand there like a great oaf. Take a chair, my son."

The Principe said, "Do what your mother says. Sit down, don't stare at our guest."

Gianni laughed, sinking gracefully into a chair. "Stare? My brother is staring too. Maybe you're staring as well, Papa."

A fleeting smile crossed the older man's face. "All right," he said. "I may stare, but I don't do it as obviously as you do. So, signorina, you had a good trip from America?"

"Yes, fine, and everything's been so wonderful here. I can't get over this view! Oh, the villa is so lovely, isn't it?"

There was a fractional silence. Then the Principe said, "The Villa Paradiso…yes, a lovely place, signorina."

Had I imagined it, or was there an undertone of contempt in his voice? I remembered Signore Predelli saying, "They don't like the name, Villa Paradiso. You must admit it's not very imaginative."

But the moment passed and they were, all of them, charming, hospitable. Francesca, amiably, asked how long I would be staying, and wanted to know how I felt about Italy. I said Italy, in my opinion, was pure enchantment. I said, "It has a wonderful, terrible beauty. It—"

"A *terrible* beauty?" Gianni repeated, looking at me with his black, velvety eyes. No man should have eyelashes like that, I thought. "I don't know why I used that word," I confessed. "Maybe just to be original."

"*Sicily* has a terrible beauty," he said. "And perhaps Napoli. But Florence? I must get you aside, signorina, and find out why you used that strange word."

"Gianni, *prego*," Francesca said impatiently. "Tell me, signorina, did you travel on one of those monstrous airplanes?"

"The 747? Yes, it was glorious. Only half filled. We had the ship to ourselves."

"I would like to go on an airplane," the little girl, Eleanora, said. She sat on the grass, at my feet, her basket beside her. "I wish that very much." She fished in her basket and offered me a dusty cookie. "For you, signorina," she said gravely. "I want you to have it."

"Thank you very much," I said. It must have been days old, was dry and musty-smelling. But I took a small bite. After all, a gift from a child.

"Is it good?" she asked.

I said it was fine, but when she wasn't looking, spit out the hard crumbs into a tissue. It was *awful*. The little girl's mother saw my subterfuge. "What is that?" she asked, looking at the stale cookie I held gingerly. "Good heavens, don't eat that ghastly thing! She saves everything! Here, give it to me, signorina."

She grabbed the cookie out of my hand. "Now, let's see what else you have in that basket, young lady."

"Nono!"

"All right, I won't touch it, then. Just…do you have any more food in there? From goodness knows what month or year…"

"I have two more cookies, that's all," Eleanora said grumpily.

"Give them to me. And don't save idiotic things like that. It's ridiculous."

"All *right!*" The child yielded the other couple of cookies, much the worse for wear.

"And don't presume to look at me like that."

The mother returned to her place at the table, while the child made a long face. Gianni said, teasingly, *"Comica, lei."*

"Non sono comica!" the little girl flashed back.

"Sì."

"No!"

"That will do, both of you," the Principessa said, but by this time Eleanora was laughing; Gianni had brought her out of her sulks. "How do you feel. Benno?" Francesca asked her husband, who shrugged and said, "Ah…*bene…*"

"Don't you think you had better get to work?"

He yawned, belatedly putting a hand over his mouth. "What time is it?"

I saw the Principe reach into a vest pocket and then, making a wry face, took his hand away. "You won't find your watch, *caro*," the Principessa said.

"No, perhaps not," he said sadly. "It is gone forever."

"Then let me buy you a new one," she said impatiently. "You keep reaching in your pocket. I don't like to see it."

She made a little sound of annoyance between her teeth, but then gave him a fond and forgiving look. "Never mind, never mind, it's all right, my dear," she said, and took his hand for a minute. Benedetto, reluctantly it seemed to me, threw down his napkin and stood up.

"All right, I go," he said, and gave his wife a peck on the cheek, waved to the rest of us and strode off. Francesca, when he was gone, explained to me that her husband worked for La Nazione, the newspaper, but that he had taken the morning off because of a headache.

The elder Monteverdi had appreciated his son's discarded newssheet; now he rose and, bowing to me, said he had been most happy to meet me, that he would see me again, and now he was going to read the day's news. "Very bad, I am afraid…it always is…"

He touched his wife's shoulder gently, as he passed her, and made his way across the lawn. I saw how tall he was, what a firm, strong-looking man, erect and almost soldierly in his bearing. And then he vanished into the house: a short while later I saw him sitting at an open upstairs window facing the garden, turning the pages of the paper.

"More coffee, signorina?" the Principessa asked.

"Yes, please."

My cup was filled. I said, *"Grazie, signora,"* and looked at the people who were sitting blithely in the shade of the large, flowered umbrella, taking their ease at twelve in the morning. I was puzzled at their indolence. Signore Predelli had given out that they were very poor. Surely Benedetto didn't support the whole kit and kaboodle with his job on a newspaper? Yet none of them appeared to have a care in the world.

I decided that they must live rent-free, that my Aunt Mercedes had demanded nothing of them, and that their sole concern was food and clothing. And perhaps Benedetto, who gambled, didn't always lose, but brought home an occasional bonanza. In any event, they seemed casual and worry-free; perhaps with the exception of Francesca, who had, if not a lean and hungry look, at least exhibited vague signs of discontent in her beautiful eyes. She seemed to me a woman who would have liked the freedom to be imperious. And in such case might be quite a demanding sort. In fact I thought I detected a certain vulgarity about her, a kind of little finger crooked in defense of origins that might not be as high-born as those of the Monteverdis.

But she was certainly wonderful looking. And had given a great deal of her beauty to her child, Eleanora, whose hair, in the bright sun, shone like gold. The child sat on the grass, her dreaming eyes almost vacant. Not stupidly so, but turned inward, as if she saw things the rest of us didn't. For a moment I wondered if she was not simply fey, but faintly retarded. There was an un-childishness about her: for a bizarre moment I was reminded of a midget, those old young persons whose deceptive, beguiling charm masks hardcore reality…they are as pragmatic and cruel as the rest of us, though we long to cuddle them.

And then she smiled up at me, her adorable mouth pink and pretty. "You are not drinking your coffee," she said.

"Eleanora, that is impolite," the Principessa said, but not sharply. Turning to me she asked me to tell her something about myself. "Are you in school still?"

"Oh no. I've been out of college for three years. I have a job, with a publishing house, which I like very much."

"Publishing?" she repeated. "That means literature."

"Not really," I answered, smiling. "I don't work for a very prestigious firm, I'm afraid. But of course I have my small ambitions. Literature, in fact, is very much on my mind. Maybe sooner or later I'll graduate from the lower depths."

"You are an admirer of fine writers?"

"Yes, certainly."

"Are you acquainted with our Italian writers?"

"To some extent yes. I've read all of Moravia. And—"

"Moravia? That's a good start. I read and re-read him. Some day I would like to meet him. He knows something about women, that man." She smiled wryly. "Most men know little about women."

"I thought Italian men knew women very well," I put in, and saw her amused glance. "The outside, not the inside," she said, lighting a cigarette. "I have read about the movement in your country, Feminine Liberation. It will be a long time, I fear, before Italian women can voice their frustrations. Bed and kitchen is the fate of women here. Bearing and raising children. Cooking. And closing their eyes to mistresses kept in charming little apartments."

"But we can get divorces now," Francesca said, popping a cube of sugar into her mouth.

The Principessa shook her head. "It won't work," she said positively. "The man doesn't want a divorce. He wants a mistress, not another wife." She swept me with an ironic glance. "They want their cake and eat it too, and it will remain that way. Divorce? No, signorina, not as in America. Things will stay the way they have for hundreds of years, because no one is really hurt by the arrangement system. It is only a slap at religion. To anger the poor Pope. But it doesn't mean anything."

She crushed out her cigarette and Gianni, laughing, said his mother was right. "We are slow to change," he told me. "And we don't really want to."

"Why should we?" Francesca asked. "Everything is fine the way it always was. I have nothing to complain about."

"If you can keep your husband from the gaming tables, you should have nothing to complain about," the Principessa said in a hard voice, and there was an angry engagement of eyes between the two women. But the daughter-in-law didn't say anything; she simply looked away, a little flushed, and in order to break a sudden uncomfortable silence I said, "I don't know whether you were told, but my aunt Mercedes left me some money in her will. It was a great surprise, because I'd never met her."

"What a pity," the Principessa said, ignoring the mention of my bequest. "We knew her for many years. She was an unusual woman, for an American."

I had the distinct feeling that she had meant to underline the word "American," and that her almost instant addition to it only served to stress it more.

"By that I mean," she went on, "she was almost *not* American, you see. She spoke Italian fluently, and preferred our language. She was not by any means an intellectual, but she was a well-informed woman. We had many talks together."

"So did we, she and I," Gianni said, and Eleanora piped up.

"And me too."

The Principessa laughed. "It's true. The signora liked children. Gianni and Eleanora."

Gianni blew smoke, from a small cigar he was smoking, into the air. When he looked back at his mother his face was angered. *"Scusi,"* he said, and I knew he was put out. "I stopped being a child many years ago. Or haven't you realized that, Mama?"

"Perhaps," she said coolly. "Perhaps."

I looked from him to his mother, and then back at him again. Well, I thought, the Principessa was fascinating, I had to admire her poise, grace and aplomb…but I certainly wouldn't want her for a mother. I put a finger through a smoke ring Gianni was blowing, and in this way showed that I sided with the son, not the mother. It was not the generation gap…it was the casual cruelty with which she had aligned him with a little girl, called him, for all practical purposes, a child.

"Now we are engaged," he said, as the smoke ring circled round my finger.

"Don't be too sure of it," I answered, and Eleanora, enchanted, tried to spiral the next smoke ring. But it was an imperfect one, and she failed.

He laughed, and took a sideswipe at her hair. She crawled into his lap. "But you know, Gianni," she said, "It's time to paint."

"Paint? Sure it's time to paint. Why don't you buy a whip, little slave-driver?"

"Whip? I wouldn't hurt you, you know that, Gianni."

He growled something and pretended to bite her nose off. "Are you a painter?" I asked, and he said yes, it was the best he could do. "But that's wonderful." I said, and he laughed. "You tell my family that," he said, and pushed the little girl off his lap. "*Per favore*, tell them that."

"My son has a talent, yes," the Principessa said, rather stiffly, and I got up, deciding I'd lingered long enough. I told them I must go, that my hostess was expecting me. Gianni got up too, and said he'd walk me over to the other house. The little girl, scrambling up at the same time, announced her intention of coming with us. I thanked the Principessa for the coffee and rolls.

"I hope to see you again, signora," I said, and she held out a hand.

"It was a pleasure to meet you, signorina."

And then the three of us walked across the grass.

"So you are going to stay here for a while," Gianni said, as we walked through the dividing gate.

"Yes, and of course I'm delighted."

On the other side of the gate, two people were kneeling in the earth. Gianni held up a hand. "Pietro," he said cheerfully, *"Come sta?"*

"Bene, signore…"

They stood up, like militiamen. A man, nudging the boy who was with him, walked over to us, the other following. Gianni held out a hand, where upon the other man, hastily wiping one of his on an earth-stained blue smock, took the slender hand.

He bowed low over it.

"This is our gardener, Pietro," Gianni said to me. "Pietro, signorina Barbara Loomis is the niece of the Contessa. She will stay here with the signora Wadley."

The gardener touched his finger to his forehead.

"*Buon giorno, signorina*"

"*Buon giorno, Pietro.*"

"This is my son, Emilio."

"*Buon giorno, Emilio*"

The boy was only about fourteen. He bobbed his head, mumbled something and then stood silent, a little flushed, and fried to pull his pants higher. They were the only clothing he wore…his lean, brown torso was naked.

"*Come sta?*" Gianni asked again.

"*Bene. Grazie, signore.*"

"You work hard, Pietro. And you, Emilio. Some day you will be rewarded."

The two bowed, their faces cast down.

"*Grazie, signore.*"

We passed them, and went on our way. There was an odd look on Gianni's face. "Good people, good people," he said, when we were out of earshot "Those who work with the earth are God's creatures. I envy them, yes, very much,"

He stopped and faced me. There was a dark, bitter expression on his face. His dark, long-lashed eyes looked into mine. "What I just said," he told me, "I have heard my father say many times. And, as I grew older, I had to hide a smile."

He laughed suddenly and looked about. "All this," he said, "the villa and its acres, once belonged to us, the Monteverdis. But times change. So you see, signorina, we take what we can, and don't question it." He laughed again. "You have very pretty hair."

His hand reached up and touched it. Lightly…but I felt a vibration going through me. "So she left you money," he said, smiling into my eyes. "That's nice, signorina."

"It wasn't very much," I said, moving away from him.

"For us, nothing," Gianni murmured. "So I would say you were very fortunate, signorina."

"But I was given to understand that, eventually, the property will revert back to your family," I said spiritedly. "Everything, in fact, that once belonged to my aunt."

He looked at me, then away from me, and then back again. "*Eventually,*" he said. "That could mean anything. For the moment, it is as it has always been. Nothing has changed."

"But—" I started to say, and he interrupted me.

"*Yet,*" he said quietly, flicking a blade of grass at his feet. His long-lashed eyes were dark and enigmatic. "Nothing has changed *yet.* But of course, from day to day, one never knows."

He put a hand on my shoulder. It felt heavy there. The little girl stood on one foot, looking up at us, at our adult conversation, which she didn't comprehend. Which I didn't really comprehend either.

"I must go now," I said finally.

He looked at me closely; his eyes, sweeping my face, were inscrutable. "Yes," he said at last. "You must go. Give the signora my regards. Tell her Gianni said hello."

He took his hand off my shoulder and walked away, the little girl tagging after him. "*Ciao*" she called back, but Gianni didn't say anything more, and I watched him treading silently across the grass, flicking a bush now and then, tall, lean, young, dark-haired, aristocratic. The two of them went through the dividing gate, and then they both disappeared from view.

"Well, here you are at last," the British voice of Elizabeth Wadley said, and her outline swam into view from the dimness of the house. "So you finally got here. Where are your bags? I didn't hear the taxi."

"I've just had a late breakfast with the Monteverdis," I admitted. "I ran into the little girl, and she took me round to their garden. I hope you don't mind."

"But not a-*tall*," she said. "Now I shan't have to do the honors, you already know them. I'm so glad you're here. I have your room ready. Come, let me show you."

She put a hand on my head. "You have wonderful hair. I had hair like that once. Both of us, Mercedes and I. Black, thick, strong. But the years fly by and then one is gray from top to toe."

She drew me in.

"D'you know," she said, in a conversational tone, "I'd give everything I have, which is substantial, to be your age again. There's no gold like the gold of youth. Some day you'll know that too. Everyone, sooner or later, comes to know that."

Chapter Five

I was installed in my great-aunt's room: it was as large as my entire apartment in New York, with french windows opening out to the garden, a variety of tables with marble tops, bureaus and an enormous armoire. There was a high, comfortable-looking bed. Mrs. Wadley fussed over me and, later, had me meet the cleaning woman, a cheerful creature in her forties, named Lucrezia, who folded fresh, fluffy towels in my bathroom, told me where there were blankets and insisted on unpacking for me.

She didn't have to insist very hard, in any event. I had gotten a headache, probably from too much sun, I thought. Or perhaps it was over-excitement; new sights, new sounds…travel was tiring… and there was admittedly something almost macabre about being in this house that had belonged to a relative I'd never known.

Everything had happened so quickly, so unexpectedly.

Mrs. Wadley came to see if I had everything I needed, chatted for a bit and then said she was going to take her siesta. She had been sitting on the edge of the bed and she got up rather stiffly, wincing a bit. She saw my questioning look and told me that she suffered cruelly from sciatica.

"One of the penalties of growing old," she said, making a face. "It's my right hip and it disturbs my sleep, don't you know. I must lie on my left side, but sometimes I forget. If you should hear me screeching, it's only that, my dear. It's like being on the rack if I land on that poor, crippled hip."

She patted my arm. "Enjoy your nap, love."

And then went off.

I had no intention of observing siesta. However, I did want to rid myself of my headache, so I took some aspirin and lay down for, I told myself, only a bit, just until the nagging ache in my head was banished.

But lying down made me dizzy, and I sat up quickly. There was a sudden, violent pain in my head, really violent, and a wave of nausea swept over me. I broke out into beads of perspiration. For a moment the whole room whirled about me and then I got to my feet, clutching at the coverlet of the bed and, making a dash for the bathroom, reeled against the door jamb. I knelt down on the cool tile and leaned over the bowl.

I retched, dryly at first, and then vomited.

It left me spent. I felt like a dishrag. Disconsolately, clutching my clammy forehead, I thought, oh my God, I've got the travel bug. On the third day of my vacation! What a kettle of fish.

At the thought of fish I retched again.

When I finally crawled back to the bed I didn't even get undressed. I kicked off my shoes and lay down. The room swam, I groaned, tears came to my eyes. I felt so sick.

I can't be sick on a holiday, I told myself, protesting. I don't have that much time.

And then I dropped off.

• • •

I woke bathed in my own sweat.

I felt weak as a cat, but my headache was gone. I sat up warily, but the nausea was gone too. Yet the thought of food sickened me, and I knew I would eat no dinner that night. Perhaps there was some clear soup in the house. I felt faintly feverish, as if I had a touch of the flu, so I took some more aspirin. They stayed in my stomach only a short time, and then sent me to the bathroom again. Only a thin stream of water dribbled past my lips…bile…I could taste the bitterness of the medicine, the aspirin.

I heard movements outside my closed door and opened it. Lucrezia was arranging fresh flowers, from the garden, in a terra cotta bowl. She was disgustingly cheerful.

"The signorina slept well? So, now you have some cheese, ham, *si?* Something cold to drink?"

"Nothing to eat," I said wanly. "But yes, I'd like a cold drink. I'm thirsty. But as for food, uh uh. It seems I picked up a little something. My stomach."

I put my hand on it. "Empty," I said. "I threw up. And I thought I was such a hardy sort."

She was businesslike and helpful. "Ha," she said. "Sit down, signorina, I bring you something." She snapped her fingers. "You will be better, fine, like that. Sit, please, I come right back."

She was as good as her word. She returned with a tray on which was a bottle of Fiucci water, a tall glass, and a small box from which she extracted two large, brownish lozenges. She filled the glass with the bottled Fiucci water, told me to open my mouth, popped the two lozenges into it and then gave me the water.

"Drink…quick…it's a good girl."

The tablets had a kind of licorice taste. "What are they?" I asked.

"Entero-vioform. Good for stomach business. In half an hour I give you two more. And now keep sitting, because I bring you some Fernet Branca. Is the best thing. Then you begin to feel better."

When she brought the bottle of Fernet Branca, she poured about a jiggerful into a small wine glass. It smelled horrid and tasted even worse. She watched me grimace and laughed. "Not nice? Americans no like. Italians? We drink if for aperitive. Is good for digestion."

For a moment I thought I'd have to escape to the bathroom again, but once the Fernet Branca was down the taste evaporated.

"Thanks, Lucrezia," I said.

"Prego, is nothing at all. Now you see, signorina, you feel better *subito."*

And after a while I did begin to feel better. I told Lucrezia so, but said I wouldn't want any dinner, and was wondering if there was some kind of thin broth in the house. She said yes, there was, and that I was very wise. "Also," she warned me, "you don't drink the tap." She tapped the bottle of Fiucci. "You drink this. Better for you, until the stomach, the digestion, is well again. Now you have your color back again, signorina."

She pulled me up. "Now go out and breathe the air. The best thing for you." She went back to her flowers. "The signora, she gets up soon anyway."

I went outside, through the french doors, into the warm, glorious sunlight. There was an umbrella table, like that of the Monteverdis, and I sat down under it, sighing. Wondering if there would be more headaches and more nausea. But after a while I started feeling more like myself again, and, stretching out in a lounge chair, closed my eyes.

It was just what the doctor ordered, I thought. This incredible sun, and the faint breeze in the trees. Oh, dear Lucrezia. She had cured me!

I was half asleep, I suppose, because first I thought it was a dream, hearing the voice calling out. In my dream someone was saying something…from far off…

I opened my eyes and heard it again.

"Ecco…signorina…"

"What?" I mumbled, and then was wide awake.

I looked over my shoulder and saw Gianni peering over the wall between the gardens. He smiled dazzlingly and raised a hand. "Hello, are you asleep?"

"I was," I said. "But someone woke me up."

"Oh, you mean me," he said disarmingly.

"What is it, Gianni?"

"Come," he said. "I paint you."

"Not in my present condition."

"What means that?"

I got up and walked across the lawn to him. "It means I have a touch of the wobblies," I told him. "Traveler's Trouble. I lost my breakfast and for a while thought I might be dying. But Lucrezia gave me some pills and something ghastly called Fernet Branca and now I feel better."

"You don't like Fernet Branca?" he asked, surprised.

"Let's say I can take my medicine like a man, and that's as much as I can offer in favor of Fernet Branca."

"Hum, that's funny," he said, frowning. "Here, we like it very much. It's wonderful for the digestion."

"Which is why I took it."

We were both leaning on the top of the brick wall. If the wall hadn't been between us, our heads wouldn't have been so close. As it was, his face was so near to mine that I could feel the waft of his breath. "Your eyelashes are too long," I said, perhaps because of a sudden silence that had fallen on us, perhaps because he was looking intently at my mouth. Perhaps because he had a certain magnetism I found a little overwhelming.

He looked a little astonished and then he laughed. "Shall we measure them, then?" he asked. "Yours and mine?" He put out a finger and swept it across my own lashes.

"Like stars your eyes are," he said.

"Nonsense."

"You come let me paint you?"

"No, but if you're painting I'd be interested to see."

He pointed to the gate near the adjoining wings of the house. "I meet you there," he said, with mock solemnity. "You won't be late?"

"Gianni, you're an idiot," I said, laughing, and we faced each other a second later at the aperture of the open gate. "So," he said.

"Right on time." He pretended to consult his watch. "American girls aren't so bad after all."

Laughing, feeling much better, I walked through the gate and across the lawn with him. There was an easel set up near the table where that morning I had had coffee. A partly finished canvas, of the view below, was on the easel, and there was a small, rickety table with brushes in jars, and a paint-smeared palette.

I saw at once that Gianni's work was excellent, strong yet sensitive. I looked at it admiringly. This young man had inherited, from his forebears, the great talent of the region. It was in the blood, I told myself, passing on from generation to generation, from century to century.

"Oh, Gianni," I said, and didn't think it necessary to say more.

"It's all right?"

"You must know," I said. "It's sublime. Oh, how I envy you."

"Florentines paint," he said negligently. "Or they work in metals, like Cellini. I would be a sculpter, sooner than this, but—"

He raised his shoulders.

"No abilities there," he said. "Just the brush, and the knife."

"It's enough," I said. "It's wonderful, what you can do."

"I can do portraits too," he said. "I paint you, yes?" He put a hand to his cheekbones. "These are good," he said, and from his own face transferred his hands to mine. "Fine planes, like marble," he murmured. "Now, when I see a face like that, if I could take the stone and drive the chisel into it…and sculpt such lovely features…"

He took his hands away.

"But I can not. It's not the same with brush and oil. The colors fade, the canvas rots. I am only a *little* painter. They won't hang me in the Uffizzi."

"Maybe they will."

He brightened a bit. "Maybe they will," he agreed. "My master, Antonioni, says maybe they will." He laughed infectiously. "You know? When I am dead for a hundred years. One hundred years from now maybe Gianni Monteverdi hangs in the Uffizi. But, *cara*, I won't know!"

He made me sit down in a chair. "I'll make a sketch of you," he said. "Quick…fifteen minutes. You want to see how you look? I show you."

"Gianni, I feel like a rag doll," I objected.

"Forget. I don't draw a rag doll. I sketch a good, pure face. And I sign it, give it to you, and some day, who knows, you make money with it."

He chuckled again. "One hundred years from now."

His laugh was deep and vital. I thought, Italian men *were* different from American men. Oh, yes. They were so damned *masculine*. They looked at a woman in a different way, had strange, exciting voices, were assertive, dominating. They were *men*, and you were a *woman*. I sat, posing for Gianni Monteverdi, and I swear I *felt* beautiful, felt like part of the sunlight, like the dazzling, multi-colored dragonfly that flitted through the air only a few yards in front of me.

Finally he threw down the crayon.

"Okay," he said. "Come and look. Tell me if you like it."

I got up and went over to the easel.

"Gianni, it's a wonderful sketch. But it's too flattering."

"Is?" He squinted at me and then looked at the sheet of sketch paper again. He shook his head. "No, darling, not at all. You look better than this." He picked up a piece of charcoal, signed the sketch with a flourish. Then tore the sheet off the sketch pad. He presented it to me.

"From Gianni," he said. "With love."

"I'll keep it," I said, "forever."

"And you think of me when you look at it?"

"Certainly."

He gazed into my eyes. Put a hand on my hair. "You could say thank you," he said, huskily.

"Thank you, Gianni."

"It's the best you can do? Say a few words?"

And, without knowing how I got there, I was in his arms. His lips were on mine, warm, questing. His hands threaded through my hair. "Caw," a bird said, in flight, and there was the tinkling knell of a cowbell somewhere. A light breeze shivered the leaves in the trees.

Agitated, I dropped the sheet of drawing paper.

"Oh, goodness, am I *de trop?*" a light voice asked, and we sprang apart. It was Francesca, in a lovely, lime-green dress, her hair piled high on her shapely head. She had gardener's shears in her hand, and a big, fan-shaped basket of rattan.

"I didn't mean to make an interference," she said. Her pretty face was mischievous.

Gianni looked sheepish. I'm sure I did too. Francesca walked past us, clicking her shears. And then her daughter, little Eleanora, came out of the house. She saw Gianni and then me, and ran over to us, found the sketch Gianni had done of me.

"Ah," she said softly. *"Bellissima. Che bella, bella."*

"Isn't it nice?" I said, when she handed it back to me. "And now I must go. My hostess won't know where I am."

"I'll come with you," the little girl said.

"Fine, darling."

She put her hand in mine. The ubiquitous basket was hooked over her arm. And when we went through the gate to the other side of the house, she looked up at me thoughtfully and then said, "Signorina, would you like to see my secrets?" She tapped the basket.

"You mean it?"

"Um hum."

"Well, then, I'd love to, of course."

"Then come, let's sit down here." She led me over to the twisted pine where the dog, Paolo, had been buried. She settled herself on the grass, asked me if I was comfortable and then opened her basket. It was shaped like an inverted garden hat, with a snap closing, and she was very businesslike about it, parting the snaps with a small fingernail, and then putting the basket down on the ground.

After which, one by one, she lifted out her treasures. There was a pair of earrings, obviously filched from her mother's vanity chest, a tiny teddy bear with one glass eye missing and a worn sticker that said JAPAN. There was also a variety of rings, cheap little trinkets made for a child's small fingers, and some little glass beads in a clear plastic tube.

A tangle of gilt chain necklets, discarded perhaps by her mother, an empty matchbox with a colored picture of San Gimignano on one side and Siena on the other, a tiny address book with a fleur de lys cover. The basket was filled to overflowing. "Oh oh," Eleanora said suddenly, and I saw a cookie like the one I had been given earlier in the day. She seemed quite embarrassed, but was mistress of the situation. "I *thought* I had given them all to Mama."

"It's all right, I won't tell," I said. "Give it to *me*."

She handed it over, a trifle flushed, and I put it in my pocket. She was about to reload the basket again when I caught sight of something else.

"What's that?" I asked.

"Oh," she said. "It's dirty, don't touch it."

"But what is it?"

"A handkerchief, that's all."

I don't know why I did it, but I suddenly reached over and pulled it out. I thought, at first that it was only soiled, as the child had said, that the brown stain was dust, earth ground into it. But it was only for a moment, and then I knew what the brown discoloration was. It was a particular *kind* of brown stain.

It was, in fact, blood.

"Why do you keep this?" I asked.

"I don't know," she said. "It was hers, that's all. I liked her. *Capisco?* She was my friend."

"Who?"

"The signora."

And then I saw the raised initials, embroidered in the cambric handkerchief. M. d'A. In one of the corners. Fine linen, crumpled and stained, with hand embroidery.

M. d'A.

Mercedes d'Albiensi.

"Where did you find it?" I asked, careful not to sound alarmed.

"When she fell."

"Fell?"

"Yes, from the ladder."

"From the ladder? What was she doing on a ladder?"

"Cutting away the vines." She pointed, indicating the top story of the house. "I was helping her. She said, 'Nora, go in the house and get me the big shears.' You know where they are, signorina? In the shed, in the courtyard. So I went there, and brought back the shears. But she was lying on the ground. I never saw someone like that, signorina. I thought her head was off. It looked like that. I thought—"

There was a quiet horror in the child's eyes.

"Then," she said, "she was dead. Mama said she didn't know it, that when you are dead you don't know it, and I was not to grieve."

My mind was whirling. I had assumed that my aunt had died of a heart attack. One always takes it for granted, with the aged, that it must have been a coronary.

But apparently it had been something quite different.

"Your mother was right," I said. "You musn't grieve. Just remember your friend with love and think only of the good times you had. And now I'd like to ask a favor of you."

"Yes, signorina?"

"It would be very nice if you would let me take the handkerchief. I know she was your friend, but she was my aunt. Would you mind *very* much?"

There was an inward battle. Finally, sighing, she nodded. "If you wish, signorina," she said, with some regret.

"Thank you very much. It's kind of you. And thanks for letting me see your secrets. You have lovely things in that basket. And now I must go and talk to Elizabeth. She'll be wondering where I am."

We parted at the gate, she with her basket and I with my drawing by Gianni Monteverdi…and in my pocket a stale cookie and something else.

A bloody handkerchief. I felt as if it were burning a hole there.

Chapter Six

I waited until that evening, when we were having *aperitivi* in the garden, to speak to Elizabeth Wadley about the accidental death of my aunt. I decided not to tell her what Eleanora had said, but rather to ask outright. In other words, I wanted to take her unawares.

I had slipped easily into calling her by her first name, and I said, abruptly perhaps, but wanting her first reaction, "Elizabeth, how did my aunt die?"

There wasn't even a second's hesitation. "Because of a total lack of sense," she said crisply. "She simply declined to admit to the infirmities of age, and went on acting like a schoolgirl. Well, she was a narcissist, of course, anyone would tell you that. She was Queen of the May for so long that she thought herself indestructible. God wouldn't *dare* let any harm come to her! She'd be alive today if she hadn't been so bloody foolhardy."

I waited, looking inquiringly at her, and she went on. "Well, I assumed, of course, that you knew," she said. "She was on the ladder, pruning some parasite vines that were choking the trees round the house. Never mind having Pietro tend to it. Oh no, she had to do it herself. Pride goeth before a fall, my dear. At any rate, she was hacking away at a great rate and the ladder must have slipped. After all, she was nearly eighty. She fell a hundred feet to her death."

She saw my face and hastened to add, "My dear, she didn't suffer for a moment. You mustn't think about it. She was never in pain. She died instantly."

"Did she bleed much?"

"*Bleed?*" Elizabeth looked astonished, and for a second narrowed her eyes with what seemed to me distaste. I didn't want her to think I was looking for sensationalism, for goodness' sake. But yet I didn't want to mention the handkerchief Eleanora had found. I said carefully, "I suppose I want to be reassured…that she didn't suffer, as you say."

"Love, it was as quick a death as anyone could ask for. She broke her neck and aside from the quite horrible position she was in, there was no other outward sign. She certainly didn't *bleed*."

Well that, I thought, was puzzling indeed. No blood on the dead woman…but a hankie stained with it in Eleanora's basket. What could one make of it?

I could hear, in the adjoining gardens, the voices of the Monteverdis, carried by the cool currents of clear air. A shriek of childish laughter, followed by Gianni's voice, told me that uncle was teasing niece, and I had to smile. I must tell Gianni, I thought, that they made a charming couple, he and Eleanora. Looking up, I saw the Principe sitting at the window on the upper story of the villa: he was communing with some bird or other in the branches of a tree which was close enough to sweep the house. The bird would cheep and then the Principe would answer it. I thought it was very touching, that while the rest of his family was gathered for their *apertivi* down below he was playing a child's game.

"Let's move our chairs a bit," Elizabeth said. "So we get the last of the sun. If you were raised in England, you'd appreciate the value of the sun. Let me help you."

"No, let me do it." I pulled the chairs out from under the sheltering umbrella and felt the sun scorching my face. I agreed with Elizabeth. If you were raised in smoggy Manhattan you also appreciated the value of the sun.

"Isn't that lovely," she said.

"Yes, wonderful."

"Buona sera," I heard someone say next door, and recognized Benedetto's voice. Evidently he had just returned from his daily

stint at La Nazione and was joining his family. I heard answering greetings, and Eleanora's delighted screech.

"Papa!"

"Yes," Elizabeth said suddenly, turning to look at me. "I do so envy them. A close family."

I thought of her, now that Mercedes was dead, sitting there night after night, listening to the sounds of affection, coveting the ties that bound lives together.

Oh, poor Elizabeth…

"Well, I must rouse myself," she said, after a long, companionable silence. "I daresay you're hungry and so am I."

Eleanora, peering through the gate, waved a tentative hand. Elizabeth waved back. "Come say hello to us, Nora."

Nothing loath, the little girl skipped across the grass. "I must go to bed soon," she confided. "I wanted to say good night."

"That was nice of you," Elizabeth said. "Did you have a pleasant day?"

"Like all the other days," she said, with an innocent wisdom. "Did you?"

Both Elizabeth and I agreed that our day had been fine, and then Gianni walked through the gate. He came toward us, looking splendid, lean and handsome in white pants, a shirt half unbuttoned and an orange handkerchief stuck in the pocket of his shirt. I thought he looked rather Neopolitan, or what I imagined to be Neopolitan. He looked me up and down, in my "little" dress that had cost a good bit of money at Saks, and smiled dazlingly.

I smiled back; a most attractive boy, I was thinking, and had to laugh at the designation. He was several years older than I. I wondered if I was being condescending…or defensive. Because I could feel a kind of pull toward him…and I didn't want to do what so many American girls did when they went to Europe, namely, fall head over heels with some vagabond lover.

"I've come to take you home," he said to Eleanora. He held out a hand and she took it. "Say good-night," Gianni ordered.

"Good night, good night…"

"Remember me to your family," Elizabeth said, her wiry hair tangling in the iron of the chair in which she was sitting. "*Buona notte*, children."

And then they went off, swishing through the grass, and vanished through the dividing gate. Elizabeth looked over at me. "Gianni has eyes for you," she said, as if she were telling me that two and two made four.

"He has eyes, I surmise, for lots of girls," I answered.

"Well, why not, he's young, and still fancy free." She got up. "And now I must fix us something to eat."

"I'll help you."

"No, *please*." She made it plain that she was averse to anyone interfering with her "joy of cooking," as she phrased it. "Don't you see," she said, in that clipped British voice, "now that I have freedom of choice I simply am so *fond* of planning meals and thinking up gourmet menus. It's the only thing I really care about."

There was an almost girlish smile on her seamed face. I sometimes feel like a child, making mudpies. And there's no one to stop me."

"It's just that I wanted to do my part," I said, and she smiled down at me.

"Don't worry about *that*," she said. "To have you here, someone to break bread with…well, I simply wish it could be forever."

"So do I," I said, knowing it was true. "It seems I don't want to leave."

"Like your aunt," she said. "You're very much like your aunt."

And then she left me, making her way across the grass to the house. I sat there, dreaming, listening to the voices from across the way. I listened, and it seemed to me that Elizabeth and I were the freeloaders, that the Monteverdis, expansive and voluble, were the masters…and we the serfs, the tenants. The low-pitched voices of the men, the authoritative tones of the Principessa, Francesca's fruity dulcet made *me* envious too, and I longed to share their camaraderie.

But there was something else. It made me faintly resentful, angry perhaps, and questioning. The property had been my aunt's and was now that of Elizabeth Wadley. But on our side of the gate was only quiet, as Elizabeth cooked our lonely dinner.

A bird flew low and winged past me, settling down, fleetingly, on the grass. I called to it and it looked up, with bright, curious eyes. I remembered the Principe, sitting at that upstairs window, having an aviatic conversation with a wren or sparrow or whatever. Now I could hear his deep voice, like that of a *basso cantante*, mingling with the others, and the window in which I had seen him earlier was dark, untenanted.

Lucrezia appeared in the aperture of the french doors, waving to me.

"*Buona notte,*" she called, and I got up.

"You're going home?" I asked.

"*Si,*" she said.

I followed her around the house, over the graveled path, and she climbed onto a little Vespa, straddling the motorcycle with solid, sturdy legs. "*Arrivaderci,*" she said, and revved the motor. Then she roared off, her coarse brown sweater ballooning behind her. The last I saw of her was a scarf at her neck billowing in the breeze.

• • •

When I went into the house again the cooking smells made me salivate. Garlic…the odor of meat fat sizzling. I was famished. I poked my head in the kitchen and said, honestly, couldn't I do something?

She looked up, abstracted. "What? Oh no, I'm getting along famously," she said, her face flushed from the range. "Would you care to play the piano again? I do so love music."

I went to the Boesendorfer and started a Brahms Ballade. I don't know precisely when it was that I saw the reflection in the glass of the many framed photographs on top of the piano. At first it was only a vague impression, that there was something wavering in front of my eyes. And then I saw the face, as in a mirror, Gianni's face, hovering outside the french doors, not knowing I could see him reflected a dozen or so times, in the pictures spread over the embroidered silk scarf.

He was peering in at me, bent slightly forward, and a funny chill went up my back. What was he doing there? Why didn't he come in, say something, make his presence known? He seemed to me to be lurking, to be spying on me...

I came to the end of the Ballade, with its final chord, and got up quickly from the piano stool. I turned and faced him, at which he straightened up, guiltily, and drew in his breath.

"Hello," I said.

"Hello," he answered, but I saw his discomfiture, though he carried it off well enough. He walked through the french doors and raised a casual hand. "You play well," he said. "I heard it, and couldn't resist—"

"It's a glorious instrument," I said. "It needs tuning, though. How about a drink?"

"Thank you, but I must get back. Another time, signorina."

"My name is Barbara."

"Yes, I know. I—"

"It's not all that important," I said, annoyed and a little bit angered. "Signorina will do, if you can't manage anything else." I knew I sounded shrewish, but I couldn't help it. Was I, then, a barbarian? An American outlander who merited nothing more than an impersonal "Miss?" Even though he had kissed me and put his arms around me? I was beginning to form a cold, crystal-clear picture of the Monteverdis. Snobs, whether you called them by title or addressed them simply as signore and signora.

He was backing out the french doors again. Smiling, with those long eyelashes, and looking more than a little embarrassed. I said, crisply, "Have a good evening."

"*Grazie, e lei*" he said, and was gone.

I could hear his soft footsteps over the grass. And looking out, saw him go through the dividing gate. Right after that there was the pop of a cork and pleased exclamations.

A party? It sounded like it. Apparently the Monteverdis were drinking champagne. Having a high old time. Poor or not poor, they certainly lived well.

I couldn't account for the spleen that rose in me. That they were out there, on the other side of the gate, laughing and enjoying themselves. I just thought, after all this was my aunt's villa…

But my aunt was dead. And the Monteverdis, apparently, weren't grieving, to any great extent, about that circumstance. They seemed to be getting along just fine. And although there was no reason for it, it made me angry…and querulous…

After all, it was still the property of someone else. Of Elizabeth Wadley. The carnival atmosphere next door made me peevish, uneasy too, and even unhappy. I wished, at that moment, that my dead aunt could have risen up from her grave, to put them in their place. Pious they were, about what a fine woman Mercedes had been…but they had forgotten. And they made merry, while she lay in her cerements…

• • •

We sat once more at the table between the windows, looking out onto the purpling evening and eating a delicious dish of clams, crisp bacon, springy mazzorella cheese and delicate breading. It was fit for a king, and I told Elizabeth so.

She accepted my compliments with a pleased smile, and ate twice as much as I did. It was almost ten o'clock when we turned on the television, and I saw at once that she had spoken the truth. The reception was horrible. "It's hopeless," Elizabeth said at last, and admitted that, anyway, it was her bedtime. I said fine with me, that I really *had* to write some letters. "I must get some things from the shops tomorrow," she said. "The larder's running low."

"May I do the shopping?" I asked. "If I can take the car…or we could both go. Whatever you say."

"You wouldn't mind going yourself?"

"I'd enjoy it very much."

"Then I'll make out a list," she said. "Oh, my, I'm enjoying having you here so much, Barbara."

She kissed my cheek. "It's such a *blessing* having you here. I don't really like being alone. It's a difficult adjustment."

"I'm sure."

I left her at the door of her room and then went on to mine. Lucrezia reported at eight o'clock in the morning, so I didn't bother to set my alarm. I sat at a table near the open windows, with a rosy lamp and my postcards, at last letting all and sundry know of my whereabouts and, rather elaborately, I fear, described the environs. There was much purple prose, for which anyone, under the circumstances, might have been forgiven. Let them know what they were missing.

I knocked off ten cards, wrote a long letter to my parents, brushed my teeth and went to bed. It was difficult falling asleep, because I was enchanted with my surroundings, intoxicated with the ineffable smells that wafted in from outdoors. I remember muttering, "Lucky, lucky girl," and then I sank into a deep sleep.

I woke sluggishly, because someone was screaming, but it was difficult to orient myself. My eyes were tight shut, my body in a kind of mummy vise. But someone had screamed. You heard it, a part of my numbed brain said. A scream in the night…you must do something about it.

Yes, some part of me answered dutifully. I must certainly do something about it.

I sank into slumber again. But conscience was nagging at me. I had heard a scream. Therefore I must do something about it.

And my eyes flew open. Someone had screamed!

I was suddenly with it. Torpor vanished, and I sprang out of bed, listened. Then stopped hesitating and reached for my robe.

The house, in the darkness, gave me to pause. I stood for a second, trying to get my bearings, and then groped my way, bumping into a few pieces of furniture, to Elizabeth's room. Because who else was in this house? Just the two of us. So it must have been Elizabeth who had screamed.

"Elizabeth?" I called, and then reached her bedroom. The door was open and the moonlight poured in. She had stopped screaming and was now swearing softly. I heard a couple of very explicit four letter words, uttered with feeling, and I went over to where she was sitting up in bed.

"What is it?" I asked, "what is it?"

She gave vent to a particularly expressive Anglo-Saxonism and then said, "It's all right."

"But what *happened?*"

She stopped muttering. "Oh, I'm so *very* sorry," she said at last. "I was sleeping too soundly, and I turned over to my right side. I didn't think I could move. I was paralyzed. It's so…damned painful."

"Oh, poor dear," I said, sitting on the edge of the bed. "Yes, I understand, you told me about it. Your hip. Are you a little better now?"

"Yes, of course. Oh, I do so hate being old! I think sometimes I should be strapped down, like someone in a madhouse. So that I don't turn the wrong way. It's such a cross! And it does hurt so…"

She put a hand to her mouth. "My dear, I apologize. I suppose I was screeching and keening. Mercedes was used to it. She simply ignored it, and so, my dear, must you."

"Let me make you some hot tea. Or rather a brandy?"

"Please don't bother. Except…you could fetch me my pills, dear. They're on the bottom shelf of the cabinet. Would you mind? The medicine chest. They're sleeping capsules…red and green."

I groped my way to the bathroom, found the light switch and then, opening the medicine chest, found the sleeping caps. There was a plastic glass on a shelf; I filled it with water from the tap and brought the vial and glass to her. By this time she had turned on a bedside lamp.

She swallowed one of the pills, drank the water, and handed the lot back to me. "You're a good girl," she said. "I'm sorry to have woken you. Everything will be all right now. I'll sleep well, and I won't turn. My mind is obedient now. I'll be fine. Thank you. Now go back to your bed."

I bent to put my lips on her cheek. "Barbara, you're a lovely girl," she said tremulously, and I shushed her. When I left she was lying on her "good" side, her left. Her nightgown was a grannie gown, a soft fleece, in a pale shade of yellow. Somehow, in spite of her years, she looked like a little girl, being put to bed by Mother. It caught at my heart. You grew old…but you wanted help, and succor…and love.

"I'll see you in the morning," I said, rubbing my cheek against hers. "Remember, I'm not far from your room. If you should need me, I'll be there. Count on it."

The faded blue eyes looked up at me. With gratitude, with trust. "Thank you, my dear," Elizabeth Wadley said. "Thank you so very much."

I turned out the light and went back to my own room. I was wide awake. I lit a cigarette, went to the windows, and looked out onto the beautiful gardens, lit fitfully by the light of a sickle moon. Thoughts were churning in my mind. The handkerchief that had belonged to my great-aunt. Stiff and crumpled with the dark residue of blood. But Mercedes hadn't bled. She had broken her neck…otherwise there was no sign.

Then what about the stained handkerchief?

And then a really electric thought came to me. The cookie. In Eleanora's basket. In the pocket of one of my jackets now…with the cambric handkerchief.

My God, I thought. My God! I had taken only a taste of one of Eleanora's cookies and shortly thereafter had been violently ill. Vomiting, nausea, a horrendous headache. Just from a tiny taste.

Most of it I had spit out. I hadn't swallowed more than a grain or two.

And the dog, Paolo, dying with a blood-specked muzzle…

Gianni had said, "He must have gotten into some weed-killer."

Weed-killer?

An animal didn't eat grass, or flowers. Except for a rabbit, or a rat. Dogs had a better intelligence. Dogs, who lived in the country, didn't die from weed-killer. They knew better. They knew *better*.

I turned away from the windows and went to the jacket I'd worn that morning. Pulled out the cookie I'd taken from the little girl's basket and looked at it.

I sniffed.

It simply smelled stale and old. I put a finger to it and then put the finger in my mouth. There was a bitter taste, a horrid taste.

Recklessly, I bit off a tiny piece of it, rolled it about on my tongue. Why was I doing this? I didn't know. I felt the crumb melting in my mouth and, suddenly scared, went to the bathroom and spit it into the bowl. But of course it had mixed with my saliva. I kept spitting and then swallowed a glass of water. Wild imaginings came naturally to me, and I was imagining at a great rate.

I faced myself in the mirror, told myself to calm down, and went back to bed, snapping out the bedroom light and then the lamp in my room. The sheets, once again, felt cool and delicious, and I drifted off.

Sweat, between my breasts and beading my forehead, woke me. I rolled over, groaning. The knot in my stomach was tying me up so that I could scarcely move. I lay, gasping for breath, the nausea flooding through me in waves. My head felt as if a pile-driver was bludgeoning it.

I fell off the side of the bed, landing with a thump, but I didn't feel the hurt of it, only that ghastly nausea, the blurred vision, and my head pounding, throbbing. *I had to get to the bathroom…*

Somehow I did. And once again, crouching on the tiled floor, leaned over the bowl. The contents of my stomach found their way into it. I thought I'd expire with the pain in my head: my eyes were tear-filled. They felt bloody.

Poisoned, I thought, sagging back, my head against the wall. Poisoned…

Like the dog.

And then I leaned over the bowl again. It was so excrutiating, so horrible. It was terrifying. It was agony.

I don't know how long I sat there, on the cold tile, waiting for the next seizure. Perhaps an hour. When I was able, at last, to drag myself back to bed, I was as limp as a sick cat. And now, I thought, as I lay in bed again, I knew. The cookies that lovely little girl had carried in her pretty little basket had been lethal. She hadn't taken them from the family table, but had found them on the grounds somewhere. There had been someone who intended the dog, Paolo, to eat them, and then die. But Eleanora had found some of them too, and had "saved" them, along with her other "secrets." Damn it, I thought, writhing with the stomach ache…

hadn't that awful person, whoever he or she was, realized that a child might come across them?

If that beautiful little girl had indulged herself…in her innocent greediness, eaten one of the cookies…

She would have died in agony, beyond help, beyond salvation…

Who could have done this horrible thing?

I had a childish thought. *I want my mother.*

No, I thought tiredly, trying to sleep. It's too late for that. I was grown up now and, anyway, she was too far away. I was on my own. No longer a child. My battles were my own, from here on in.

I turned, and sighed. I was so tired, so damned tired. And because of that, at last I slept. My limbs relaxed and my eyes closed. Until the bright sun, streaming into my room, snapped my eyes open.

Warily, I moved a bit. I was weak, but my headache was gone and so was the nausea. Mainly, there was anger. Why should anyone have wanted to harm a little dog? For what reason, to what advantage? I remembered Paolo's glassy eyes, the foam of blood on his muzzle. It could have been me too. It could have been that lovely little girl. Or anyone.

But why, but why?

Chapter Seven

When I was dressed I hunted up Lucrezia, who was coddling eggs in the kitchen, and told her that I had a recurrence of my "tummy trouble." Thereupon I was given some more entero-vioform, another dose of Fernet Branca and inside half an hour was feeling considerably better.

After breakfast, in the garden with Elizabeth, we discussed the household needs and, as she had said she would, had made out a list. She gave me the address of a *drogheria*, a grocery, where I would find fruit and vegetables, and that of a shop which sold meat and fish, both on the Via Cerretani. Then she gave me the keys to the little blue Lancia.

I had my map with me, but first I had to drive down that precipitous, winding road. At least *I* was driving, and could go at my own pace. I was ultra-cautious, particularly when the road opened up, where there were no houses, to show the plunging descent far, far down below. There was only a two-foot road barrier, of stone, between my car and the seemingly bottomless chasm below. But there were no other cars, though I honked warningly at each curve, and then I was at the foot, on terra firma, going through the old city wall, breathing normally once more.

I crossed the river at the Ponte delle Vittoria, drove along the Lungarno and found myself heading for the Via Tornabuoni, close by. I had made a quick decision…impulse, perhaps, but on the spur of the moment I decided to talk to Signore Predelli about the things that were puzzling me. I had, yes, a vivid imagination, was well known for it…but it hadn't been imagination that had made me deathly sick after a taste of a cookie given to me by a small child.

Signores Predelli and Pineider should know what had happened…after all, they were the executors of my aunt's will. I parked the car in the Piazza di Trinita, and then crossed over to the lawyers' building. It was only a little before eleven, a cool, clear morning, though the sun was rapidly heating up the day. I went up in the lift and the girl at the desk recognized me at once.

"I don't have an appointment," I said, "and if they're too busy to see me I'll understand. Would you ask, please?"

"Certainly, signorina," she said, and picked up the intercom. A second later Signore Predelli came through the door to the waiting room and kissed my hand. When I was in his office he sat me down, and after some small talk I told him what had happened.

"First the dog," I said. "And then me. Well, what do you think?"

"And the *child* had them?" He looked stunned.

I nodded. "She had something else too," I said. "A handkerchief of my aunt's, covered with dried blood. I took it away from her, along with one of the cookies, as diplomatically as I could." I said again, "What do you think?"

After a silence he said, "I don't know. It certainly seems very strange to me. Could I see the handkerchief, please?"

Of course I didn't have it with me, and I told him so. "It's in my room back there," I said. "But you can take my word for it, the discoloration on the handkerchief is unmistakably blood."

I got up. "I mustn't take any more of your time. But, in a way, you and your partner are my only links with home. So I thought you should know. In case—"

When I heard what I said, which echoed in my ears, I was shocked. *In case...*

In case I should meet with another "accident?"

But it was ridiculous! What had happened to me was gratuitous, and had not been intended for me. I became brusque. "For some time now," I said, "I've had the impression that you and your partner know something I should know too. Don't you think it's time you told me about it?"

He looked greatly astonished. "But, signorina," he said, "I can't imagine what…your conjectures astound me…you are on holiday, and should be enjoying yourself. When you go home, I hope you will take many snapshots with you, of Firenze, and show them to your family. Meanwhile, simply have a good time. Why not? This is a lovely city, a beautiful countryside."

"Yes," I said. "But with a dark side. I think you know what I mean."

"No," he said, smiling tentatively. "I don't."

"If you don't, or pretend not to know, I have nothing more to say." I got up. "And obviously I must settle for that."

He rose with me. "Yes," he said, smiling gently. "It is better that way."

"You're practically telling me to keep my nose out of things," I said angrily.

"I didn't mean to convey that," he said, and his face was still and quiet. "Of course, signorina, if something should happen that might upset you, you must get in touch with us immediately. It goes without saying that my partner and I have your interests at heart."

"How kind of you," I said ironically, and a few minutes later was out on the street again. I was annoyed and disturbed…Signore Predelli hadn't leveled with me. He had put questions into my mind, where there were already questions. But he hadn't resolved any of those I had come to him with.

If something should happen that might upset you, you must get in touch with us immediately…

Exactly what did it mean? Only that there were reservations in his mind…and it was as far as he cared to go. Damn them all, I thought and, driving recklessly, braked my car and parked it in the Piazza de Repubblica.

I got out and went to the shops Elizabeth had told me about. I bought the supplies, stowed them in the back of the car and then walked over to the Piazza san Giovanni and sat down at a table in one of the numerous sidewalk eateries there. I ordered a *tosta* and *birra*, a lightly-toasted sandwich with Italian ham and springy cheese, and a small bottle of beer.

It was right across from the dead center of the city, the Duomo, with its gilded dome, the octagonal Baptistry, and the divine belltower Giotto had designed. I was in the very heart of one of the loveliest cities in the world. The beer was cold, the sandwich tasty. I was just lighting a cigarette, after finishing this light lunch, when I heard the loud voices. They came from a table rather far away and at first I didn't think anything about it, as Italians are ebullient people, with a tendency to throw their arms about dramatically and, when excited, raise their voices to several decibels.

Then, astonishingly, I recognized one of the men at the table. There were, in all, three gentlemen seated at an umbrellaed table which was, as a matter of fact, at an adjacent cafe. Several cafes ran together, side by side, and all appeared to be doing a thriving business. But then, of course, I knew by now that Italians enjoyed food, the company of others, and the sun, so the outdoor restaurants were always filled to overflowing.

It was Gianni's brother I recognized, Benedetto Monteverdi. And watching him, with the others, I realized that there was an argument going on. That the two other men were tormenting him and that he was leaning back in his chair looking red-faced…and a little scared.

I surveyed the other two men. They were very dark, swarthy, with heavy black hair and hard eyes. They seemed to be Neopolitan, or Sicilian. They didn't look, truth to tell, very *nice*. The word "Mafioso" came to my mind. Dramatizing again, I told myself.

But then…

A knife embedded itself in the wooden handle of the umbrella. I could see the cold flash of steel, even hear the thud as it hit the wood, splintering it. Several persons, near me, gasped. By now the group was the focus of attention. At a table near that one, a man rose, leaning forward, staring…and a waiter stood, at attention, neither moving from left to right, simply looking fixedly at the three men.

I had a glimpse of Benedetto's face. It was ashen, quiet and still, with a gray pallor. Then suddenly the man who had thrown the knife pulled it out, folded it within itself, and stuck it into a pocket. He and his friend got up, said something in low voices, and walked away.

Benedetto Monteverdi was left alone.

He looked quickly about, saw himself the cynosure of all eyes, looked down again, pulled a wallet from his pocket, threw down some lira on the table, and walked quickly away.

The table was empty now.

I paid my own bill, left a three hundred lira tip, and went back to the car. If I had wanted drama, I had had it today. I was sure those men had been threatening Gianni's brother, and then I remembered something Gianni had said.

"Drinks too much, gambles too much…"

Yes, I thought. It could be like that. Benedetto, at *ecarte* or *chemin de fer*, had lost great sums of money. And now he couldn't pay. What did a newspaperman earn at his job?

He couldn't pay.

It was all wildly dramatic. That knife, flashing in the sunlight, quivering in the wood spine of the striped umbrella…

I drove back home. By now, I had become used to the snake-like road. Almost casually, I managed the steep ascent. My trouble was still when the stretches of open territory loomed into view… and I saw the abyss below, the yawning chasm thousands of feet down. It made me dizzy, and I concentrated on *not* looking at it, but instead keeping my eyes strictly on the dusty road I was driving.

Practice made perfect, I told myself, zooming into the gravelled driveway and pulling to a stop: I had done it once again. "That's a frightful road," I told Lucrezia, the first person I saw, and she smiled sympathetically.

"*Si,*" she said, grinning at me. "You were frightened?"

"Scared out of my wits," I admitted. "One wrong turn and it would be the end. Doesn't it ever bother you?"

"No, because I know it so well," she answered, and asked if I had seen the other car in the driveway. I had. "To whom does it belong?" I asked.

"An American gentleman. He's outside, with the signora."

I went inside, loaded with my parcels. She helped me carry them into the kitchen, planking them down on the marbleized butcher's block.

"Nice meat," she said, turning the steaks and fillets over. "*Bene,* signorina. Very good."

"Your stores are marvelous, I spent a fortune. You say there's an American gentleman here?"

"*Si.* From New York City."

"Well, what do you know?"

"Like you. You are from New York City."

"Don't remind me," I said.

"*Prego?*"

"Nothing. Just a joke. Is he good-looking?"

Her lips reared back, showing the gums. She giggled, and pushed at my arm.

"And young too," she said.

"Well, that sounds interesting."

"I put these away. You go out now."

"All right, Lucrezia. See you later." I went out of the house and, walking across the lawn, saw Elizabeth standing near the wall that overlooked the valley. She was gesturing, looking very pleased with life in general, and beside her was the visitor from New York.

I wasn't particularly surprised. As soon as Lucrezia had said it, I had a pretty good idea of who "the American gentleman" was. Neither was he taken aback. We smiled at each other, in a confidential way, as Elizabeth introduced us. That he didn't want me to let on that we knew each other was evident from the quick, almost imperceptible shake of his head.

"This is Mr. Fox, from America," Elizabeth said. "My guest, from America too, Barbara Loomis."

We shook hands and, while the three of us walked and talked, Peter exclaiming over the beauties of the place, I was busy thinking. I felt I knew what had happened. Signore Predelli had passed on my morning's confidences to Peter, who—there was no longer any doubt about it—was interested, perhaps as much as I was, in my great-aunt's demise.

And now he was here.

I remembered something I should have tagged earlier. That first night at the Buca Lapi, the fragments of conversation between Peter and Signore Pineider.

"How far is it?"

"Six kilometers."

And Signore Predelli had said to me, speaking of the villa, "It's only about six kilometers."

It had rung a bell but only subliminally. The repetition of the words. I was impatient to talk to Peter alone, and my opportunity came only a short while later. It was way past siesta time, and when Lucrezia came out, like a stern parent, and told Elizabeth that she must get her rest, my hostess agreed.

"I shall leave the honors to you," she told me, and said she hoped Mr. Fox would come again. And then, as she disappeared into the house, Peter turned to me with a grin and said, "It *is* a small world, after all."

"I suppose Signore Predelli mentioned my presence here. Oh yes, I saw you with Pineider, that first evening, at the Buca Lapi."

"*Did* you. Well hello again, Barbara."

"And to you. What's your business here? No, don't tell me, because I've already guessed. You're an investigator for an insurance company in the States, and you're doing a routine check on my aunt."

He laughed. "Certainly not. Your aunt's life was not insured. Her assets were so enormous that insurance, of that kind, would have been ridiculous. And by the way, Predelli and Pineider don't know I'm here. I mean here talking to you. I didn't think it necessary to tell them that."

"So you do have some connection with my aunt's estate."

He nodded and I said, "I thought so. How about a drink, Peter?"

"You mean a real one? Not a sickish-sweet Strega?"

"I went shopping today and stocked up on gin. I can mix a mean martini. Twist or olive?"

"Olive by all means. It sounds wonderful."

"I'll be back in less time than it takes you to sit down and make yourself comfortable."

"Life," he said, gratefully, "can be beautiful."

I left him stretching his legs and leaning his head back against one of the garden chairs. And whipped up a heady pitcher of my very special Big M's. I put a few of the cheese croutons on a tray and went out again. "Now tell me," I said, when we had wished each other a cheery *Buona fortuna*, "what's this all about?"

"Nothing much." He sipped his drink, said it was first rate and then put his glass down on the table. "I came here to unsnarl a few snarls. I represent an American firm of lawyers; we've been handüng some of your aunt's affairs. Of course it's an infinitesimal part of her holdings. The bulk of the estate is here, in Italy."

"Did you tell Mrs. Wadley who you were?"

"No."

"Why?"

"There was no reason for it."

"You're being mysterious," I objected.

"Not really."

"Not really? Then why didn't you introduce yourself as *yourself*?"

"Because I am not concerned about Mrs. Wadley," he said. "It's you I'm concerned about."

I laughed. "*Concerned* about me? In what way?"

He looked at me speculatively. "Did you or did you not get sick eating a bit of cookie?" he asked me.

"They told you about that? Yes, I did. But it wasn't meant for me. It was meant for the dog, obviously."

"They also told me about the bloody handkerchief. Of course I'm only a lawyer, and it doesn't have any bearing, per se, that your aunt might not have died a natural death."

"Falling off a ladder isn't exactly a natural death, Peter."

"At least we agree about that," he said dryly, and a sliver of chill touched my spine. So I hadn't been dramatizing. Others wondered about it too.

"What are you thinking?" I asked curiously.

"I'm not sure. My thoughts are muddy, and I have very little to go on. Just that it seems to me, inescapably, that Predelli and Pineider are peculiarly tight-mouthed about your aunt's death. You know, when you deal with people, you notice expressions, glances exchanged, that kind of thing. You can't help it, it's in you, you *see* these things. It's nothing more than that. Or it wasn't, until I learned about the dead dog and the handkerchief the little girl had. And then I began wondering."

He shook his head. "No, I began wondering, vaguely, on the evening I had dinner with Signore Pineider. He told me, in essence, that there were more things in heaven and earth, Horatio, than—"

He smiled. "Well, he said people in his business had many stories to tell and he could imagine that I had some of my own.

I said yes, of course, and he went on to remark that, for example, this Contessa d'Albiensi…there was a story there, a very dark one, he felt sure, but that it could, of course, be in his imagination, only he didn't think so. "I've often thought of writing some of these episodes into a book," he confided to me. "But of course I don't care to be involved in a libel suit."

"So you—"

"Yes, so I began to get interested, and tried to worm it out of him, but no go. Then I found out that a girl I'd met on a bus trip from Rome to Florence was the niece of the woman in question, and then started being *really* interested."

He leaned forward. "That's why I haven't returned home."

"Oh, really?"

I didn't mean to sound flippant. But I suppose it seemed that way to him, because he looked at me once more with that thoughtful lift of his eyebrows. "Look, Barbara," he said. "I don't like the sound of it. I don't cotton to the idea of you, with your bright eyes, spending a week or two weeks in this place. I thought instantly, there's something odd and something strange, and there she is, with her bright eyes, in that *particular* situation, which doesn't sound right to me."

He picked up his glass again, sipped, and put it back on the table with a little bang.

"Do you still have the cookie?"

"Yes."

"And the hankie?"

"Yes, of course."

"May I take them with me? I'd like to see if I can find out anything."

"I have no objection to that."

And then I told him about that morning. "I was sitting at a table in the Piazza san Giovanni, having lunch, and suddenly I heard a commotion. I looked up and saw one of the Monteverdis, Benedetto."

I told him what had happened. "I felt as if I were in Sicily. Vendettas…knives…well, I could scarcely believe my eyes."

"What do you think it meant?"

"Gianni says he gambles. I presumed it was that. He couldn't pay and they were threatening him. It was ghastly, like a crazy Italian film. Knives! Imagine it…"

I left him looking a little grim, went into the house and fished the cookie and handkerchief out of the pocket I'd left them in. When I went out again, Peter was pouring himself a second martini. He looked up and grinned.

"I'm putting you on notice," he said. "Any girl who can make drinks like these is someone a man doesn't want to have slip through his fingers. If you don't mind, I'd be grateful for your Manhattan telephone number. I'm thirty-four years old and have never been to the altar. Just haven't found the right party. Until now, that is. Or do you have a fiance lurking in the wings?"

"No," I admitted. "Just dinner dates. If you're interested in dinner dates, Peter, I'm available."

"Famous last words," he said, with a nice smile. "That's the way it starts. Dinner dates. And before you know it—"

I laughed, liking him. "For the moment," I murmured, "it's dinner dates. If you're really going to be here for a while longer, I'd love to meet you at a *trattoria*, for grog and grub. Meanwhile, here are those little items which I pass on to you for whatever you can find out. And if you don't mind—"

It was then that I saw the shadow.

On the other side of the gate someone was standing. Someone whose shadow was cast across the emerald lawn, limned by the hot rays of the sun.

There was someone just at the other side of the gate.

Peter saw me stiffen.

His back was to the gate. He didn't move, but signalled me with his eyes. I signalled back. "Stop talking," my eyes transmitted. "Don't say anything more."

He sipped his martini imperturbably. I puffed on my cigarette. Whoever was standing there must have been alerted by the sudden silence. The shadow foreshortened…soon there was no more shadow left. The person who had been posted at the gate had gone quietly away.

I wanted to know who it was.

I got up quickly. Went over to the gate, looked through it. But I was too late. There was no one in the other garden. There *had* been someone, but not now. Whoever it was had gone quickly into the house. There were only the trees, the bushes, the birds flitting busily through branches, the deserted iron table, the scallops of the flowered umbrella flapping idly in the breeze.

I went back.

"Were we talking loudly?" I asked.

"I don't think so," Peter said thoughtfully. "Someone was listening?"

"Yes, someone was listening."

He crushed out his cigarette, drained his glass and got up. "I'm off," he said. "I'll attend to this." He patted his pocket. "Meanwhile, keep the faith. I'll be in touch."

He looked down at me. *"But,"* he added, "if for any reason something bothers you, you're to call me at my hotel."

He reached in a pocket and pulled out a small pad. Taking a ballpoint pen from another pocket he wrote something on a slip of paper.

"The telephone number of the hotel," he said. "My room's 416. Okay?"

"Okay."

We crunched our way around the house, where he got into a car he had rented, and drove away, the dust of the road churning up, and then I went back to the garden. I had another martini and looked, narrow-eyed, at the gate. Who had it been? Whose shadow was it? Who'd been listening to Peter and me?

We were almost whispering, I told myself. No one could have heard what we'd said. We'd been talking softly…I was sure of that. I looked at my wrist-watch. It was two thirty. There was a compulsion to do what everyone else did here, get into bed and sleep the mid-afternoon hours away. I shook myself and said no, I won't give in to it, it's sick. I came from a pioneer country. We didn't waste three hours of a day in bed…

No.

But I stood in my room and looked at the bed. Why not? All Florence was sleeping: why not me? I heard a sound and realized, by my swift reaction to it, that I was more keyed up than I had thought. I gasped, turned, and saw a shadow across the lawn just outside my french windows. God in heaven, what now? I asked myself and stood stark still.

The shadow came closer.

I started backing up toward the closed door of my room. And then I heard the voice.

"Signorina?"

It was Gianni. He was suddenly there, a shadow no longer. He stood there, outside, looking in at me.

I found my voice.

"What do you want?"

"If you were in bed for siesta I wouldn't have disturbed you," he said. "But you're not in bed, and you're dressed. So may I come in?"

Angered, still feeling the shock of seeing the second shadow, I snarled at him. "Gianni, this is my room, do you mind? Please go away. At once."

"Oh?" he said, and made a silly face, like a small boy being punished. In the most ridiculous way his lower lip quivered. His dark, liquid eyes were forlorn. "Bye bye," he said in a broken voice. "I'm sorry, *cara*."

"It was you," I said, walking toward him. "Wasn't it?"

"It was me what?" he asked.

"Listening to my friend and me in the garden."

His eyes were bright and curious. "Who is your friend?"

"Don't try to con me. We were talking and then I saw someone next door…in *your* part of the garden…standing at the gate."

"Well, that someone wasn't me," he said, shaking his head positively. "Anyway, what's worrying you? He was making love to you, your friend?"

"How do you know it was a he?"

"Because I saw him." His eyebrows raised disdainfully.

"An ordinary sort of guy," he commented.

"I'm not interested in your evaluation of my friends."

"Look," he said, putting a hand on the side of the open window. "Let's have a nice afternoon."

He started to come in. I put out my arms, warding off his approach, and I had a moment of weakness…or terror. I didn't trust Italian men, and I didn't trust Gianni in particular. I remembered the moment in his arms…but that had been in the freedom of the outdoors.

There was a moment of darkness, as the sun went under a cloud, and with lithe, long steps he reached me.

"Gianni, don't," I protested, retreating.

"Don't what?"

"Stay where you are. Please."

He looked at me. "So you feel it too," he said. "This thing between us."

"I don't feel anything of the sort," I cried. "And I certainly didn't invite you in here. Go away, *capisco?*"

He looked at me and then, suddenly, there was no smile on his face. Without the smile his face was almost severe, was grave, almost forbidding. "I'm to go, then," he said quietly.

"Certainly you're to go. You're in my bedroom. You've no business to be here."

He nodded. "You're right, I've no business to be here."

"Then…just go," I said peremptorily.

And then, as quickly as it had fled, the smile came back again. I saw now that there was a cleft in one cheek, as in Eleanora's, and that it deepened when his lips curved in that particular way. "Tell you what," he suggested. "I'll go, yes. But I will wait for you. *Si?* I'll take you sightseeing. To San Miniato, I think. A good view of the city. You haven't seen it? All right, you'll see it with me."

He looked at a watch on his slender wrist.

"Ten minutes?"

"No. I'm going to take a nap."

"No you're not," he said pleasantly. "You're going to take a drive with me. You can sleep when you are old. Come as you are, don't change. Wash your hands and brush your hair if you like. I will be waiting, at the front of the house."

He touched a finger to his forehead, pushed back a lock of dark hair and walked away, springily, on the balls of his feet.

I won't, I thought, sitting down on the bed. And then found myself springing up, going to the mirror. I brushed vigorously, watching my hair fluff out with electricity. I finished with that, dusted some powder over my sunburned nose and, reaching for a fresh blouse, got into it. When I went round to the front Gianni was standing beside one of the cars I had seen in the Monteverdi's side of the driveway, a small, shining-clean Alfa Romeo. "Oh," he said, looking up. "So you decided yes."

"Why not? I was invited and I accepted. Did you think I'd cop out?"

"Cop out? What does it mean?"

"What does it matter, since I didn't? Well, are you going to open the door for me?"

He laughed, and threw it open, saw me in and then went round to the driver's seat. The car roared and snarled when he turned on the ignition, and then we were driving down the narrow road the way taxi drivers took it, practically on two wheels. I put a hand on his arm and told him to take it easy. "*Prego*, Gianni…"

He laughed, pressing down on the gas. I saw his beautiful, long-lashed eyes in the overhead mirror, dangerous and wonderful, and somehow enigmatic. I didn't know what to make of Gianni, or what to make of my vagrant feelings for him. I didn't trust him… but sitting beside him, I knew I didn't want to be anywhere else.

He questioned me like a drill master.

"You like Firenze?"

"Very much."

"You like Italia?"

"Enormously."

"You like the villa?"

"Yes, it's lovely."

"You like the Monteverdis?"

"Of course."

"And me, Gianni?"

"I think you're most interesting."

His eyes flashed sidewise, engaging mine. He laughed again and made a pass at my hair, tangling it. Then he questioned me again.

"You live in New York City?"

"Yes, I was born there."

"You have sisters, brothers?"

"No."

"None?"

"I had a sister who died as a child."

"Oh," he said, serious for a moment. "I'm so sorry. Forgive me, *cara*."

"Well, it was a long time ago."

After a while he said, "So it is just the three of you?"

"The three of us?"

"You, your mother and your father."

"No," I said. "I don't live with them. I have my own flat."

He raised astonished eyes, then picked up my left hand. "You are not married? But still you don't live with your family?"

"No. Many girls don't, when they come of age. In my country, that is to say."

"Here," he said, "it would not be so. Until marriage, the child lives at home."

"Every country has its own ethos," I said.

"True, true. You told my mother you had a job. In literature."

"I told your mother I had a job, but that it wasn't precisely 'in literature.' It's very commercial, the house I work for. I'm an editor."

"Like my brother," he said. "He also is an editor. Only for a newspaper. But it's the same, probably. Yes?"

"Yes, I guess more or less the same."

"Why are you not married, signorina?"

"It will come in time. You're not married, either. Why not?"

He said substantially the same thing as Peter had. "When I find the right girl."

"Well, it's the same with me," I answered. "When I find the right man."

Waiting for a light to change on the Lungarno, he picked up my hand, stroked it, and bent to touch my nose with his own. "You see," he said teasingly, "I didn't meet *you* before this. Now I met you and I like you and maybe I will change my mind, who knows?"

"About what?" I asked sedately.

"*You* know, what we were talking about," he said, laughing and, the light changing, plunged forward again. "Last night I dreamed about you, did you know that?"

"How could I know that?"

"I thought you might guess," he said. "Wake up and think, oh, goodness, Gianni dreamed about me. It could happen that way, perhaps, that the other knows about the dream."

"Well, I didn't."

He turned and looked at me again, half serious, half jesting. "Anyway, I did dream," he said.

"That's interesting. Aren't we supposed to turn in here?"

"Yes, how did you know?"

"Because the arrow says San Miniato in this direction."

"Quite right," he said, and we drove up a steep hill.

Our ride had taken us along the Lungarno, where we had crossed the river at the Ponte alle Grazie, turning into the Piazza Peggi, from whence we were now wending our way, circuitously, to the Piazza di Mechelangelo, passing a campanile of ancient times. When at last we reached the very summit of the hill, Gianni parked the car; we got out and he led me over to a waist-high brick wall.

"Now you see the beauty of Firenze," he said, pointing downward. "Now you see my beloved city. Is it not wonderful?"

If I had thought the vista from the villa exquisite, it was nothing compared to this. I longed for the wings of a bird, so as to fly, free and unencumbered, over the loveliness that lay below. Every spire and dome, tower and turret, was like a miracle: what lay below seemed fairyland, a shimmering mirage, like the wondrous landscape in the pure and guiltless mind of a child. The Arno, a ribbon of gold-glazed blue, pierced the distant city like a needle. I caught my breath and Gianni bent to look at me.

"Is it not fascinating?" he asked.

"Yes."

He looked closely at me. Embarrassed, trying not to show my emotion, I turned away. But he tipped my chin up.

"I think you like it very much," he said simply. "I think you feel it in your heart, the way you look at it So then don't go back. Stay here. Why do you want to go back?"

"Oh, don't be silly," I said irritably…irritably because I ached *not* to go back. I pushed his hand away. "Let's go into the Cathedral."

"All right," he said, and as we went up the long, steep flight of stone steps, I could hear the organ thundering away. It was Bach, a toccata and fugue, and the interior of the cathedral was cold and eternal: it had been there for hundreds of years, for another hundred of years would give solace to troubled hearts. I had a moment of fierce anger at the practice of obsolescence in my own country. Nothing was sacred, nothing inviolate…nothing…

We walked down the aisles, our footsteps echoing hollowly on the marble. Dim, vaulted, the rose windows blazing in the afternoon sun, the beautiful old church was a reminder of beauty that could never die, or ever be extinguished. Eternally tranquil, promising life everlasting for those who ached for it, the vast stone edifice was a reminder that man had a soul, and was not totally venal. It was a sanctuary, and the message outside, on one of the great oaken doors, proclaimed it.

To all those tired, or weary in heart, or forsaken, these walls are shelter and retreat, for meditation and prayer. All are welcome, whatever their faith or denomination. Pax vobiscum.

As we left, the organist, having finished his Toccata and Fugue, switched to A Mighty Fortress Is Our God. And to those majestic strains we left, Gianni and I, and went down the stairs again, dozens of stone steps, hundreds. His hand was in mine, helping me, and I didn't question it. I wanted the warmth of his skin, human warmth, right now…right now…

At the bottom of the steps he tipped up my chin again. "So," he said. "You are a romantic. A poet. I like that. Your eyes are filmed with emotion. I like it, signorina. Very much."

"My name is Barbara," I said crossly, trying to blink the idiotic tears away. "Why can't you call me that?"

"I will," he promised. "Yes, I will. Only, let's be frivolous now. There's a cafe just down the hill. Come on, darling, smile again."

The roadside cafe looked like a picture postcard, with trellised vines overhead that were heavy with purple grapes. There were flowers in abundance, in stone pots, and it was well patronized, with American, British and German tourists, and a sprinkling of Italians. We had sandwiches and beer.

Four o'clock vespers rang out, and a contingent of novices, white-robed, moved in stately fashion from the cathedral, carrying banners, to the Baptistry beyond. Birds sang in trees and a camera flashed, capturing a party of people at an adjacent table, along with me and Gianni, forever.

I looked at my watch. "Getting late," I said regretfully. "I'm afraid we'll have to go."

"You are right," he said, sighing, and called for the *conta*.

"It was a nice afternoon," he said, as we left.

"It was a beautiful afternoon. I'll never forget it. Thanks, Gianni. Thanks very much."

Chapter Eight

When we got back, Lucrezia was just leaving. She told me that Elizabeth and I had been invited next door for dinner. She gave Gianni and me a sly look and, behind his back, even winked at me. I winked back, not to be outdone. She climbed onto her Vespa and, before starting the motor, called to me, "Signorina, the evening is quite cool. Perhaps you had better take a shawl for the signora. In the top drawer of her dresser."

"All right," I called back, and told Gianni to go on ahead. "You won't take all night?" he demanded, a hand on my arm.

"No, I *won't* take all night. I just want to wash my hands and get Elizabeth's shawl. Tell your family five or ten minutes, I'll hurry."

I went into the house, lit a few lamps for cheer, ran my hands under the water and didn't bother to do anything else. There was this to say for a sunburn: makeup wasn't required. I regarded my bronzed face in the mirror and told myself I was quite a dish. Then I snapped out the light over the washbasin, made my way to Elizabeth's room, found a shawl and was about to step into the garden when something caught my eye.

I don't know why, but I noticed.

Of course Lucrezia had much work to do in this large villa, even our half of it, and I had observed that surfaces were not entirely free of dust. It didn't matter. The only thing I was ever fearful of, in my Manhattan apartment, was roaches. I had been lucky in that regard, but part of it was due to eternal vigilance. A little dust didn't break my heart so long as vermin were not present.

It wasn't the dust that bothered me. It was the fingerprints in the dust. Oh, not well-defined prints…simply the marks of hands in several places. Marks that left little, clean trails. It gave me a kind of electric feeling, those little trails. It signalled something to me.

I looked about and saw the streaks everywhere. On a desk, a lowboy, a bedside table. My bachelor apartment had been broken into once, and it was just small signs that had stayed in my mind. Little nothings…but amounting to so much in the final analysis.

Abruptly, I left Elizabeth's room and went back to my own. And yes, they were there too, those ghostly fingerprints, etched, eerily, on the top of my vanity, my writing table and my bureau. And then, alerted, an uncomfortable pounding in my chest, I checked my armoire.

It was closed, as usual, but was not closed *correctly.* That is to say, the left hand door had a catch at the top which, unless one slid it up, left the door a tiny bit ajar. It was ajar now, although that very morning I had secured it firmly. I was not the most compulsive person in the world, but living alone in a rather small flat I had learned the value of good housekeeping.

And I knew I had slid the catch earlier.

Someone had been in my room. And in Elizabeth's room. I was sure of it.

Looking for something?

But what?

I stared at myself in the mirror over the washbasin, smoothing an eyebrow thoughtfully. What in the world could someone expect to find in Elizabeth's chaste room…or for that matter, in mine?

I didn't know, couldn't imagine. But I was sure, was positive, that someone had been roving through our bedrooms, and it made me uneasy.

For the moment, only that.

But I knew that when night fell, and I was all alone in this room, with someone able to step in over that low sill, as I slept —

That I would be intimidated, apprehensive, and that I would find sleep difficult to come by.

"Now this is ridiculous," I said to my reflection, and snapped off the light. I picked up my handbag and stepped outside onto the grass, making my way to the gate and then through it. I was greeted warmly, asked my preference in the way of drinks, and Elizabeth asked me if I'd had a good day.

"Gianni said the two of you went to San Miniato."

"Yes, it was gorgeous."

"A superlative view," the Principe said. "I was told it affected you so that you had tears in your eyes."

"Did he say that?" I asked, annoyed. "It was simply the sun in my eyes."

The Principessa smiled. "You seem to have a Latin temperament," she said. "Don't be ashamed, it is a sublime sight up there."

"But you haven't done any shopping yet?" Francesca asked, looking surprised, even shocked. "But our shops are…one day you and I will go together, *si?* You would save money, without the import tax."

"Yes, I really should buy a few things," I agreed, and asked where her daughter was.

"In bed and, I hope, asleep," Francesca said, but as I sat drinking my *aperitivo* I caught sight of a golden head at the upstairs window where earlier I had seen the Principe with his newspaper. The little girl was leaning out, her chubby arms on the sill, looking down at us, and I had a recollection from the distant past of myself sitting on the stairs of our duplex, gazing through the carved railings of the banister at the incoming guests…the beautiful dresses, the perfume drifting upwards…

She saw me, made a round "O" with her lips, and instantly retreated. I didn't let on.

Dinner was served just as the dying day turned into a violet dusk. The Principessa, like any ordinary housewife, brought out the meal on a cart, wheeling it across the lawn. Both Gianni and Benedetto jumped up to help her and, pushing a strand of her iron-gray hair back from a faintly perspiring forehead, she took her place at the table and began serving. It was a simple meal but a delicious one, veal in a butter sauce, with small artichokes, following an Italian equivalent of Coquille St. Jacques. In an ice bucket were two bottles of wine. I said I was becoming fond of wine with my meals and asked what I was drinking. The Principe said, with a smile, that it was simply a *vin ordinaire*, from one of the nearby estates of the *campagna*.

"It costs very little," he admitted. "But we prefer it to more sophisticated vintages."

It was a fine evening. Elizabeth, who sat across from me, told me I was *so* wise not to wear my dresses that dismal new length. "With legs like yours it would be criminal to hide them. I myself used to be admired for my legs."

"Oh, now you are fishing," Gianni said teasingly, and kissed the back of her hand. "You have better legs than most women half your age."

"My legs still aren't too bad," she said pridefully, and I realized she was a bit tipsy with the wine. "But the rest of me is porridge. Oh well, what does it matter? I've had my day. Now it's your turn, you young people."

"Here's to legs," Benedetto said, raising his glass. Francesca giggled and said, "Now, now, Benno."

"Oh, but I like legs," he said, and sank his teeth into her shoulder, at which she giggled again and pushed him away.

"*Animale...*"

He said something in a low voice and she raised her eyes to heaven. "This is a sinful man," she cried. "I married such a *terrible* man..."

"Gianni, would you see to the espresso," the Principessa said, and Gianni got up to lift the urn from the cart. It was dark now, with only the candles flickering, and a firefly or two jetting through the dimness with a flash of gold. The valley below was a blaze of light, winking from window and turret, and the air was like gossamer.

No wonder Mercedes had never left, I thought. No wonder...

Chapter Nine

I was sitting in the garden next morning, after breakfast. Elizabeth had excused herself, saying that she had slept badly the night before and would take a few winks to make up for it. I had my face tipped up to the sun and was thinking about buying a bikini at one of the shops down the hill when I heard a voice. Opening my eyes, I saw Francesca standing at the gate of the dividing stone wall.

I said, "*Buon giorno*, Francesca," and she lifted a hand, said, "May I?" and without waiting for an answer came through the gate and toward me.

I saw at once that she had been crying. Her sherry-colored eyes were puffy and, perhaps noticing my scrutiny, she reached in the pocket of a handsome, trailing robe and put on a pair of oversized sunglasses.

"Do I disturb you?" she asked.

"No, of course not. Please sit down. I was just being lazy, and trying to get as brown as a berry. This Italian sun really does the trick."

"Yes," she said, but vaguely, as if she had only half heard me. She sat down on one of the white garden chairs, reached in a pocket again, brought out a packet of Italian cigarettes and pulled one out. She found a match, lit the cigarette, and was unable to hide the trembling of her hands. I did my best to cover up for her.

"Would you like some coffee? Lucrezia, I'm sure, has a fresh pot. No? That's a beautiful thing you're wearing, Francesca. I haven't bought anything yet. I was just thinking about a bikini or two. You said you'd tell me what shops to go to. Oh, there's an ashtray. How is your dear little girl? I can't tell you how charming she is. I'm sure you're very proud of her…"

And, chattering, I watched her trembling subside. The fingers that held the cigarette were steady now. She pushed the gigantic sunglasses, tinted a bright blue, further up her small, chiselled nose and smiled at me.

"I suppose you can see I'm upset," she said.

"Why…"

She shook her head impatiently. "Of course you can. It must be quite evident. You see, signorina, I'm—"

I waited, while she puffed at her cigarette and then, with a set jaw, crushed it out in the ashtray.

"It is very…*difficile,*" she said, her voice hard and brittle. She bit her underlip. "I wake in the morning and ask myself why I should go on. Yes, signorina, I am at my wit's end. Women have not the easiest of lives. They watch and wait…and who knows where it will all end?"

She leaned forward, tense.

"Perhaps they will kill him," she said in a strangled voice.

I sat up quickly. "What do you mean?" I asked, and she pushed the enormous sunglasses up her tiny nose again with an impatient hand.

"My husband is in serious trouble," she said.

I remembered the two men at the outdoor cafe in the Piazza san Giovanni. The knife quivering in the wooden shaft of the striped umbrella. The drawn look on Benedetto Monteverdi's face.

"In what way?" I asked quietly.

I saw her teeth set, and for a moment her round, pretty, dimpled face looked gaunt and almost ugly. "He gambles," she said tightly. "And he needs money to pay. He needs almost two million lira."

I tried to convert the lira into dollars…but I was no mathematician, and at last I had to ask, "How much is that in American currency?"

She didn't hesitate for a moment. "Three thousand dollars."

The rapidity with which she answered gave me the message. I cringed, offended and shocked. Because of course I knew why she had come here this morning. Her husband was in trouble…all he needed to be free of it was three thousand dollars. The American signorina must be rich…perhaps the American signorina could save the situation…

"Ask her," I could hear Benedetto saying, as if I'd been a fly on the wall of their bedroom, tossing and turning in the bed. "I have to pay. Ask the American girl. For God's sake, help me, Francesca…"

And, drying her tears, she had gathered up her courage and come to me.

A prince and princess, and their sons and daughters, scrounging for money to pay *gambling debts*…

She began talking fast. "The money would be paid back," she said. "Every penny. He has learned his lesson. Benedetto won't do it any more. I know he won't."

She looked suddenly terribly pathetic, and no longer tried to stem the tears that flowed from her eyes. Her head, bowing like a flower beaten down by wind and rain, drooped sadly. "Just…if we can manage to…to pay this debt…"

She raised her head. Took off the sunglasses, let me see her drowned eyes "I have to save him," she said brokenly. "The family…if they knew…"

I was terribly disheartened, because her pitiful mission was hopeless. I could no more lend them three thousand dollars than I could fly to the moon. I didn't have three thousand dollars. In my savings account back home there was eleven hundred dollars I'd saved by scrimping, doing without, economizing in every way possible.

And it was mine. I'd earned it. It wasn't nearly enough, in any event, for the squaring of Benedetto's gambling debts. It wasn't even half the amount.

And that this woman had been desperate enough to tap a total stranger for a loan.

I was horribly disillusioned. Sorry too, for poor, pretty Francesca, with her swollen eyes. Sorry for a family who lived, in some way I didn't know about, on the good will of my late aunt. I thought, she must have provided for them, *in interim*, in some way. Until they came, after Elizabeth Wadley's death, into the gigantic estate Mercedes d'Albiensi had left.

Which was so near, and yet so far. Elizabeth might live for another ten years. Meanwhile, although the Monteverdi family had free tenancy (I supposed) and perhaps a pittance for their food and upkeep, they had nothing put aside for a rainy day, such as Benedetto's gambling debts. And, teary and distraught, one of them approached a total stranger for a loan of three thousand dollars.

My voice sounded thin. I said, "I'm so awfully sorry, Francesca. I wish I could help, but I can't. I haven't anything to offer. Just a job is all I have. It pays my rent and utilities and food. I don't have any money. I will have some money, left to me by my aunt, but not for months, or maybe a year, or maybe more than that."

I saw her shrink into herself. She believed me, I guess. She had lost her pride, apparently, because she said, "Oh, I told him that. I just had to—"

A sob escaped from her.

"I just had to try," she said in a muffled voice. "I don't know what will happen."

She got up, leaned against the table for a moment and then, blindly, sticking on the sunglasses again, started to walk away. I was terribly disturbed. I got up too, and walked with her to the gate. The poor thing was shaking like a leaf. "Can't Gianni help?" I asked. "Can't—"

She turned to me. "Gianni? Gianni is an honorable man. He doesn't gamble, he doesn't waste. He doesn't have anything, except when he sells a painting, or a watercolor. Ask Gianni? I should have *married* Gianni! Then I would not spend all my time crying, lose my looks, feel wretched…ah, signorina, you don't know! I want to die! Because living like this—"

She put a hand over her face. I looked at her heaving shoulders. "Francesca," I said, but she moved past me. Lifting her head again, her face drenched, her eyes wild, she asked my pardon. "You must excuse it," she said. "I shouldn't have done it. You must excuse me. You must—"

I put a hand on her arm. "But I feel terrible," I said. "I'd like to help…only I can't. Isn't there anything…anything else I can do? I mean—"

She wrenched away from me and her eyes, darting at me were desolate, yes, but also vindictive. "There is only one way," she said. "And if not that, then nothing. I must go."

"But Francesca…" I put a hand on her arm again. "I wish I could—"

She looked at my hand as if it had been a snake, and then writhed away from it. I felt as if my touch had dirtied her, that she felt that way, that my flesh, on her flesh, was hateful to her. Her eyes blazed for a second: her face, looking into mine, only inches away, bore an expression of contempt, even detestation.

"I am sorry to have bothered you," she said in a clear and distinct voice, and the intonations were so filled with anger and fury that I quailed, drew back. And leaving me with that horrid, hateful look, she plowed over the grass and went through the gate. I heard her footsteps swishing through the grass on the other side.

I stood, shaken, and then went into the house. I sat on the edge of my bed, trying to calm myself. Asking me for money! A stranger…where did she think I would get the money she wanted? I was just, after all, a young woman, with a small inheritance that wouldn't even come to me for quite a while. Why should she tap *me* for a loan? And, failing to get it, look at me with such loathing?

Why?

Why any of it, I thought impatiently. Why any of it. The questions in my mind, and the bloody handkerchief and the bit of sweet that had made me so sick and the enigmatic looks on the faces of Predelli and Pineider? Why the fingerprints in the dust, and Peter Fox staying on because he was *concerned* about me...

The sun blazed in and I was suddenly weary of it. I got up, drew the french windows together, slatted the blinds. I ripped off my shirt and shorts, pulled down the counterpane and lay in darkness, trying to put thoughts out of my mind. Years ago, as a child, I had done this. After a punishment, or a scolding by a teacher at school. Now I must forget about it, I had thought then, and so I thought now.

I must forget about it, and when I woke it would be in a different frame of mind.

Chapter Ten

I woke when Lucrezia knocked on the door of my room. "Signorina?"

"Come in."

She opened the door and told me that someone was on the telephone for me. "A gentleman," she said, withdrawing.

I got up, slipped into a robe, went out to the drawing room. Lucrezia wasn't there: I assumed that she had gone away to give me some privacy. I picked up the receiver, and it was Peter Fox.

He said, "Can you talk?"

"Yes, I'm alone."

"Well, then. Listen, Barbara, I've been busy. I had the cookie tested at a lab. You're a very fortunate girl. Let me tell you what the lab technician read to me from his Pharmacology textbook. I wrote it down. Are you listening?"

"Yes, of course, what is it?"

"I'm quoting," he said. "Quote: *Nux vomica was introduced into Germany in the 16th century as a poison for rats and other animal pets. Its use as a rat poison persists to this day and, as an ingredient of "rat biscuit," strychnine is a source of accidental poisoning in children. Strychnine was first employed in medicine in 1540, but it did not gain wide usage until two hundred years later.*"

"Unquote," Peter said. "You nibbled on a rat biscuit, damn it, for God's sake, and it's a wonder that little girl didn't pop one into her own mouth,"

I said, "Are you sure?"

"Yes, I'm sure," he said impatiently. "It's a reputable laboratory, of course I'm sure."

"But it wasn't meant for me," I said quickly. "It was for the dog." I thought about it. "But, Peter, maybe it was meant for rats!"

"There's a slight possibility of that," he conceded. "However, if it was used habitually, why didn't the dog eat a biscuit before? Animals are canny; besides, if that kind of thing was in regular usage on the grounds, your aunt, or Elizabeth Wadley, would have conditioned the dog. It doesn't wash, Barbara. Nevertheless, you might, discreetly, ask about it."

"I could pump the gardeners," I said.

"Do that. And now there's something else. I had a test run on the handkerchief. As I said, I've been busy. And I found out something puzzling. Your aunt's blood type was O, which is what most of us have. I consulted the coroner who was called in when the Contessa died. But the blood type on the handkerchief wasn't the same. According to the technician at the lab, there are three other types, to wit: A, B, and AB. The type on the handkerchief was AB."

"But that's—"

"The same type as Mrs. Wadley."

I looked nervously about, but I was still alone, and rather breathless. "How do you know Elizabeth's blood type?"

"She was in the hospital a year and a half ago, for tests. I found that out and learned, at the same time, her blood type. The same as that on the handkerchief that was in the little girl's basket."

"But what could it *mean?*"

"I keep asking myself that," he said. "I have two theories, both of which might be way off base. Listen, can we have dinner this evening?"

"Yes, I'd like to see you, since all this throws me for a loop. Why don't I meet you at the Piazza de Repubblica? I'll take the car, and tell Elizabeth I'm visiting with someone I met in Rome. Wouldn't that be better than having you come here? She might begin to wonder."

"Agreed. Yes, I'll look for you, under the arcades near the post office, at seven this evening."

•••

He was pacing up and down and, as I walked toward him after parking the car, I saw several ladies of the evening wiggling their hips in his direction. I thought why not, Peter was a most attractive young man. That I didn't vibrate to him meant only that there was an element missing, that his ilk was over-familiar to me. He was just another American man with good credentials, and I seemed to be looking farther afield.

I *am* like my aunt, I thought and, rather than surprise, I felt a kind of warm pleasure. That I wanted to be different, to be not run of the mill but apart from the regular and the mundane. I thought of Gianni's dark, long-lashed eyes, and wished —

Well, never mind, I told myself. I was having dinner with a nice, decent American gentleman, and I would enjoy myself. He saw me approaching and held out a hand.

"How are you, Barbara?"

"Fine, have you been waiting long? I'm a bit late."

"Don't think about it. I was early. I thought we'd go to Sabatini's. Okay with you?"

"Fine with me."

He tucked my arm in his and we walked, through the noisy, crowded, narrow streets to the Via Panzani. It was a large *ristorante*, with four dining rooms and an authoritative maitre d'hotel, who handled the stream of guests with an experienced hand. We had a drink at the bar, while waiting for a table, but the din of voices surrounding us made confidential conversation impossible. We simply sat and drank and at last were summoned to a table, where we had another drink and then studied the menu.

"I know what I'm having," I said.

"The scampi?"

"Yes."

"Me too. And now we've decided that, how are things back at the ranch?"

"Puzzling."

I told him about the finger tracks in the overlay of dust, and about Francesca's proseletyzing visit. "It's all very complicated," I said. "And then *you* call about blood types. I don't know what to think."

"I do," he said. "I think you should get out of there and stay somewhere else."

"You mean leave the *villa?* Why, I wouldn't think of it! Why should you even suggest such a thing?"

"Because I feel your timing's bad. There's something going on there…or there *was* something going on there. And—"

"But it's nothing to do with *me!*"

"I'm not so sure."

I laughed. "I'm only a *visitor!* Peter, you've been a wonderful friend, finding out those things, and of course I'm intrigued with the status quo. It's a funny little mystery and it certainly has me wondering. But I'm only a bystander. Of course I'd like to get to the bottom of…whatever there is to get to the bottom of. It's a very natural interest in my great-aunt…wouldn't you feel the same? But as for me, why I'm only a—"

"A visitor," he said, interrupting. "Yes, I know, you said that before." He drained his drink glass. "How long do you intend to stay?" he asked.

"For another week."

"By that time I'll be gone. This is not a vacation for me, it's a business trip."

"I shall certainly miss you."

"I wonder." He put his glass down and looked into my eyes. "I simply dislike so much going home and leaving you here. I'll worry. Can you understand?"

I knew, then, that he was "putting me on notice," as he had said before. That he was drawn to me, and was letting me know it. A few weeks before it would have meant something to me…a man like this, interesting, solid, substantial and, yes, kind. But all I could think of was Gianni's dark eyes.

"Don't you dare worry," I said. "What is there to worry about? I've earned this vacation and I mean to enjoy it."

"All right," he said. "But if I want to worry, I'll worry. I take it as my right."

And at the concern in his eyes, the frown on his face, I felt a little humbled. If I wanted, I could hold out my hand and then, I was almost sure, he would declare himself.

But all I could think of was Gianni's dark eyes…

•••

When we left Sabatini's we walked to the Via Porta santa Maria, for cognacs at an outdoor cafe. There was a pianist, on a platform, a violinist who strolled, and a singer. It was very *Italian*. I was asked my preference by the heavy-browed fiddler. "La Golondrina," I said, and Peter laughed. "That's Spanish, Barbara."

It didn't matter. The Spanish number was played, and sung, bravura style. The melting strains filled the night. *"Buona notte,"* several patrons said, in a friendly way, as we left, Peter throwing down a few thousand lira on the table, a big spender. We would be welcomed with open arms if we showed up there again, I knew.

"It was a beautiful evening," I said, as we walked back to the Piazza de Repubblica. "Thank you, Peter. For a glittering, enchanted evening."

"There's a song," he said, and his eyes, very serious, gazed into mine. "Some enchanted evening. Once you have found her, never let her go…"

And all I could think of was Gianni's dark eyes.

Chapter Eleven

I was at the villa shortly before eleven. I parked the car in the driveway, let myself in and, after locking the front door, went to my room. I got out of my clothes, brushed my teeth and, with a last look at the fragrant night outside, crawled into bed. I was asleep almost immediately, and dreamed of a dark-eyed young man with a cleft in his cheek. He was holding my hand as we floated over the Arno, like two birds, and he was pointing out the places of interest.

"There's the Duomo and see, signorina, the belltower? What time do you want it to be?"

"I want it to be forever," I said, my fingers entwining with his. "No real time, just forever, Gianni."

"Then it shall be so," he said, and held up a hand. And time stopped, and the sun became an immovable bright spot in the sky, and the earth ceased its revolutions, and it was forever, eternal, without ending. "Thank you," I said, kissing him. "Thank you, Gianni, for making me immortal."

Chapter Eleven

When I went out to the garden for breakfast, the gardener Pietro and his son Emilio were working away. There was a ladder, atop which was the young boy, slicing away at vines that covered the roof of the villa. Elizabeth, sitting at the garden table, was looking up, her eyes haunted. I thought, she's remembering, remembering Mercedes on top of the ladder. And then the fall.

"… in a quite horrible position…"

Mercedes, lying on the ground, with a broken neck.

She saw my comprehensive look and shrugged. She knew what I was thinking. And I knew what *she* was thinking. "Have some of this lovely jam," she said quietly. "It's quince, rather difficult to get here. But as I said, that superb British shop has *everything*."

I spread some on my roll. "Isn't it good."

But I couldn't keep my eyes away from the ladder. Pietro was calling up instructions to his son. And the boy followed directions. Finally he climbed down, and the two wheeled a barrow, filled with lopped-off vines, round the side of the house. When they had gone I pushed back my chair. I couldn't help myself; that ladder held a terrible fascination for me. I stood beside it and looked up. Pictured myself there, on the topmost rung…and the ladder swaying under me…the plunge downwards…

I turned abruptly.

And my organdie morning coat caught in a nail that protruded from the ladder. It made a big rip. "Damn," I said, feelingly. It was a costly bit of frou frou; I had bought it for my trip.

"Serves me right," I said to Elizabeth. "Look what I've done." And then I saw the blood. I parted the torn material and looked at my arm. The nail had gouged my skin, and blood was running down my shoulder.

"Here," Elizabeth said, and handed me a linen napkin.

"I can't use that. I'll go inside and get some tissue." The new robe, I could easily see, was ruined. Torn, jaggedly, and stained with blood. So much for the money I spent on it, I was thinking disconsolately…and then I happened to look up and see Elizabeth's face.

It was as white as chalk. Well, she had a naturally fair, English skin to begin with. But now…well, she had a kind of paper pallor…and she looked a little sick.

"Good heavens," I said. "It's only a superficial cut, Elizabeth. I'll just go in the house and attend to it. I'm just upset about my robe."

I walked across the lawn, briskly, holding my hand over the bloody gash. I must ask Lucrezia for some iodine, I was thinking. That nail was rusty.

I was already inside the house when I stopped abruptly.

Thoughts are visual: in my mind, as vividly as if it had been painted there, I saw the stained handkerchief of my aunt. That darkened bit of cambric…

Oh, I thought. Oh…

When Mercedes had fallen from the ladder.

And hadn't bled, had broken her neck, but hadn't shed blood. Yet Eleanora had found her handkerchief, stained with red…

I stood, in the dimness of the house, thinking. My mind was racing on, reconstructing a scene I hadn't been part of, but picturing it, *seeing* it…

Supposing that Elizabeth had reached out, looking up and, angered by an earlier squabble, enraged at her own impotence, taking revenge…

I saw it clearly. Elizabeth putting a hand out. Shaking the ladder, in a moment of frenzy…sending my great-aunt to her death. And had caught her hand on the rusty nail.

When the woman with the broken neck lay on the grass, Elizabeth, whimpering incoherently, had snatched up Mercedes's handkerchief and bound her bleeding hand in it…

And now she was mistress of the manor.

Her face, when she saw my reddened arm…

Like a specter. The red mouth a gash in her shocked face…

I had Lucrezia cauterize my arm. It hurt like the very devil, and then she put a bandage on it. I didn't go outside again. I didn't want to look into Elizabeth's face. I was afraid of what I might find there. I said I would lie down for a while, and I did. There was no formal lunch hour, and it wasn't until siesta, just a bit after twelve, that I left my room. Lucrezia said, cheerily, that the signora was napping, and how was my wound?

I said it was throbbing a bit but that I guessed I'd live. And quietly, I went out to the garden, where I heard, from the other side of the gate, the sound of a child singing. I knew it was Eleanora, and I knew I wanted something from her. The ladder was gone, for which I was grateful, and I went into the house again and changed into the peignoir I'd worn that morning.

Then I went back outdoors and looked through the gate at Eleanora. I had taken something from my handbag, as a lure, and now I whistled softly to the child. She looked up, saw me, and scrambled up, skipping through the dividing gate.

"Signorina…"

"What are you doing, dear?"

"Sleeping." Her mischievous eyes challenged me. "I am *supposed* to be sleeping. But I don't care to."

"I have a present for you," I said.

"For me?" Her eyes were eager. "What?"

I held my hands behind my back. I had a Kennedy half dollar, saved for years…but if it would serve the purpose now, I could bear to part with it. "Want to guess?" I said.

She stood on one foot.

"A turtle."

"A *turtle?*"

"Because I want a turtle." But she surmised it was not that. How could I have known she wanted a turtle? She had a certain hard realism. "A doll?" she hazarded. "A picture book?"

"No. Come here, darling, I'll show you."

She followed me, her yellow dress starched and ironed. Her sturdy legs would one day be beautiful, as she would be. Those exquisite, flowery eyes…

"Where shall we sit?" I asked her.

"Under Paolo's tree."

"All right."

We made ourselves comfortable there, underneath the twisted pine. And then I gave her the silver half dollar. She drew in her breath. "Ah, *che bella, bella,*" she said. She didn't have any idea of what it meant, but I told her. "One of our presidents," I said. "And when he died, they——"

She listened to the story, big-eyed. "It's not for spending," I said. "It's for keeping. It's the nicest thing I could think of to give you."

"Ah, signorina," she breathed. "This is very, very nice. *Grazie, grazie.*"

"Can you visit for a while?"

"Certainly, signorina."

I talked aimlessly for a bit, telling her about American children, American schools, and so on. And then switched the conversation to the subject of my late aunt.

"You liked her, didn't you, Eleanora?"

"Yes," she said and then, forthrightly, "Even so."

"Even so? What does that mean?"

"Because *they* didn't."

She had opened her basket again, and was fondling the silver piece I'd given her. "Who didn't like her, Eleanora?"

"Mama, and Papa, and Nonna and—"

She dropped the half dollar and parted the grass to pick it up again.

"But *you* were fond of her."

"Yes, and Gianni too." She looked up, a lovely, bright smile on her face. "I love Gianni, don't you?"

"He's a very nice person." I feigned indifference. "It's too bad the others didn't like your friend the Contessa."

"Yes, too bad," she said, but philosophically. "But of course she took everything away from us." She lifted her head, serious. "They said she did. She had no right to have our house. But signorina, we live here! I am very happy. Why didn't they want her here?"

"Maybe because once upon a time this whole place belonged to your family," I said gently. "Don't you think it must have been that?"

"But it belongs to us," she said reasonably. "Doesn't it?"

I wasn't interested in educating a child in the whys and wherefores of property ownership. I simply said, "I'm sorry I never met your friend the signora. You know, she left me some money. Wasn't that nice of her? And I had never even seen her. What do you think of that?"

"*Bene,*" she said. "That's good, signorina. I am glad for you. Everyone is always worrying about money."

"Who?"

"Mama and Papa. Mama cries, and Papa gets angry." She shrugged, not really interested. "What happened to your *toga,* signorina?"

She was looking at the tear in my robe, as I had intended her to. "I tore it on the ladder," I said. "Isn't it a shame?"

"Oh, *male,*" she said, looking sympathetic. "So pretty it is. Oh, you mean the nail. Yes, the signora hurt her hand too. When I came back, with the shears, I saw that she had hurt herself. She was bleeding."

"You mean the signora Wadley?"

"*Si.* She had the handkerchief on her hand."

She shuddered, gritting her teeth. "Ugh…I don't like to see all that red, do you?"

"No."

The little girl sighed. "It was a very bad day. Mama screamed. And Gianni said, *Mama mia!* He went down on his knees. And then Pietro came, and Emilio. Nonna was walking up and down, saying, 'Get the doctor…'"

"Do you mean that when my aunt died, there were other people around? Your Uncle Gianni, and the gardeners, your grandmother?"

"But, signorina," she said, looking at me as if I had a screw loose. "The signora was dead, *capisco?* Of course everyone came."

"Yes, of course," I said. "Your grandmother and your Uncle Gianni, and the gardeners, and Mrs. Wadley."

"And Paolo," she said. "He barked, and then he was crying, the little dog." She looked into the distance. "It was very bad, signorina. Afterwards I cried, but Mama said I was not to think of it."

Her winy brown eyes looked up at me. "But I think of it," she confessed. "I thought her head was off her body. It looked that way."

I hated querying her, bringing back what was best forgotten, but there was one last question. "Incidentally," I said, "you remember you gave me a cookie the first morning I was here?"

"Yes," she said, looking up.

"Where did you find those cookies?"

"Here," she said. "Under the tree here. They were nice, like little mushrooms. Paolo was eating them, but I took some for myself. But then Mama took them away from me. So did you, signorina. So I have no more left."

"You're sure of that, Eleanora?"

She looked astonished. "But, signorina, you yourself took the last one. Don't you remember?"

"Could I see your basket, please?"

She frowned, displeased. "I have already shown you my secrets," she said.

"But you see," I said carefully, "the cookies might have looked pretty, but they were not the way they looked. Can you trust me? Please do, Eleanora. I don't want you to be hurt. And I would like to know, for sure, that you have no more of them left."

"Why?" she asked, her eyes wondering.

"Because I'm your friend. Believe it. Let me see your basket."

She pursed her lips, thought for a moment and then, sighing, opened the basket, held it toward me. *"Ecco,"* she said, like a little school marm. "Now you can see, signorina."

And together, we peered into the basket. One by one the treasures were lifted out. She exclaimed, enthusiastically, over a snake bracelet, which I hadn't seen before. "Ah, *che bella, bella,*" she cried, holding it up to me. "Mama didn't want it any more."

"It's lovely."

There were no more cookies. I satisfied myself about that. That the child was in no danger was a relief. "All right, thank you very much," I said. "*Grazie, mille grazie.* Now you can close your basket again."

"I *told* you," she said, reasonably, and snapped it shut.

I changed the subject. "So you like my present?"

Her face brightened. "I love it! It is American, *si?*"

"Very American. I was saving it for myself, but I thought, well, there's someone else who might like it. You, Eleanora. And so now it's yours."

She put a lotus-like hand on my arm. "We are friends, no?"

"Yes, we're friends."

I gathered her into my arms. Her warm, pliant body fit nicely there. Her lashes swept my cheek. When I released her, she plucked a flower from the grass, held it under my chin, said something I myself had said as a child.

"Do you like butter, signorina?"

"Yes, very much."

"I know, I know! Because there…" She held a finger under my chin…"it is yellow. So it means, signorina, that you like butter."

"In my country," I said, "if we find a four leaf clover it means good luck." I turned over on my stomach, parting the blades of grass.

She laughed delightedly. "Here too it is so," she cried. "*Ecco*, signorina…we hunt for it, no? Maybe you find one, maybe me. Then we have the good, good fortune. Oh, I hope so, signorina, I hope so…"

• • •

I called Peter Fox when I went inside. He wasn't at his hotel and so I left a message. He phoned me back shortly before three. "I thought you might like to know that I learned a few things today," I said, and told him about the rusty nail on the ladder, and that I had gashed my arm on it. And I described Elizabeth's white face.

"Oh?" he said, and fell silent.

"What do you think?"

"The point is, Barbara, what do *you* think?"

"I don't know. I'm fond of Elizabeth. But of course she was the sole inheritor of my aunt's estate, aside from a few small bequests. And she's blooming, I will say that. Oh, but that makes me feel like a traitor! Forget what I said."

"Aside from the blood on the handkerchief, do you have any reason for suspecting Mrs. Wadley?"

I surprised myself. "Suppose I did," I said. "I've come to the conclusion that my aunt was not the most wonderful of persons. Apparently she was a miser, holding the reins in a tight hand, and

Elizabeth is eating as if she never had a square meal in her life. She seems happy as a lark. Could she have jostled that ladder? I find myself not unsympathetic. After all, the late Contessa was almost eighty."

"Well," he said mildly, "you seem to have a criminal bent. Would *you* have jostled that ladder if you'd been under the thumb of an imperious woman?"

"She was imperious?" I asked curiously. I had come to that conclusion myself, but was wondering why Peter had used the word.

"She was imperious," he said firmly. "I've talked to shopkeepers, tradespeople, bank tellers. Take my word for it, she was a first class bitch. Oh, I'm sorry. She was your flesh and blood, wasn't she?"

"Only on my mother's side," I said foolishly, and laughed. "Heavens, Peter, she was very far removed. You're not hurting my feelings."

"It would be the last thing I'd want to do," he said. "But Barbara, you've just told me something that might have a bearing on all this. It's given me an idea. Maybe we can go farther afield than Mrs. Wadley. I've just thought of something."

"What?"

"The ladder," he said.

"Yes, all right, the ladder…what *about* the ladder?"

"Did it ever occur to you that—"

Suddenly I knew that someone had come into the room. It was just a slight sound, but I knew at once that I was no longer alone. I said quickly, "I must go now. I'll talk to you again."

I hung up quickly.

And looking over my shoulder saw Elizabeth Wadley standing in the doorway. She had a peculiar look on her face. "To whom were you talking?" she asked.

"Just a friend of mine…"

"Was it that American?"

I tried to dissemble, but was struck by her expression. It wasn't accusing, nor was it angry...or displeased. Her face was simply quiet, speculative.

"Yes," I said. "I was talking to Mr. Fox."

"I was almost sure of it," she responded. "All right, Barbara, let's go outside. I think you and I had better have a long talk."

Chapter Twelve

I followed her out to the garden. We sat down, under the trees, and she lit an unaccustomed cigarette. "First of all," she said quietly, "I overheard your entire conversation just now. Everything you said to Mr. Fox. And I know he's not just an ordinary tourist. I'm not senile, not by a long shot. I know what was in your mind this morning, when you hurt your arm. You gave me *such* a look!"

She puffed on her cigarette without inhaling and waved away what I had started to say. "No," she said. "You don't have to speak. You think I gave the bloody ladder a bit of a push, don't you? Well, you're wrong. I had my hand on it, yes. I'll tell you why. Because I tried, unsucessfully, to save your aunt's life."

She described an arc with her arm. "You and I sit here sheltered by leafy trees. I was sitting that way on that particular day. Unseen by anyone, hidden by the trees. Mercedes was up on the ladder. I was very angry at her. Being such a fool. Like a sixteen year old girl…showing her legs…almost eighty and proud of her legs…as I said, a narcissist. Furthermore, we'd had a terrifying argument earlier in the morning."

She snorted. "With the people you're fond of, there's always an element of ambivalence. We were, in a way, strange bedfellows…I, luxury-loving but without a penny to my name. Mercedes rich as Midas but no appetite for the good things of life. From one end of the year to the other she didn't have her things cleaned, went about in disreputable pants and baggy sweaters stained with grease spots. There was never enough to eat. I was dependent on her for my very toothpaste. "You must tell me whenever you want something," she always said. I would sooner have died. If I wanted something…if I *desperately* needed something, I told Lucrezia, and she bought it out of the household money."

There was a rather long silence. Then, "I suppose I did, in a way, come to hate her," she said in a low voice. "She was a jailer, in fact…a benevolent despot…but just the same she reigned supreme, and I—"

The leaves, shivering in a cool breeze, trembled in the trees, and the hour, three o'clock, bonged out from the belltower in the center of Florence. I sat and waited. There was nothing for me to say, nothing was expected of me. A woman was baring her soul to a stranger.

She went on. "But much as there was resentment in my heart, I loved Mercedes. Can you understand? She was my life. It can be a half life, a sometimes unhappy life. But a life. I'm lost without her. I go through the motions, coddle myself, eat heartily and know I'm a rich woman. But what have I really got? Nothing, nothing. My beloved enemy has left me."

"Elizabeth," I started to say, touched to the quick, but she stopped me. "Just the same," she said, "you're right, Barbara. Mercedes's death was not an accident. Someone did push the ladder. And I know who it was. I saw it. I saw the hand reach out. Mercedes tried to save herself, but—"

She gripped the top of the round garden table. "In that moment I *was* Mercedes, trying not to fall, trying to stay alive, trying to—"

She put a hand over her mouth. "When I reached her it was too late. I couldn't get there in time. I gripped the side of the ladder and tore my hand on the nail."

"Elizabeth," I said, stunned, "why didn't you tell me this before?"

"Because it's over and done with. Because nothing can bring Mercedes back. Let the dead bury their dead, as I have. Well, I feel dead, yes. Stuff myself as I will, I'm stuffing a corpse. I hope I don't live too long, but it would be just my rotten luck…"

She gave me a somber look. "It's just, when I heard you talking that way…thinking I could have killed my friend. Why, Barbara, I can't kill a fly on the wall. I make poor Lucrezia do that."

"Then who was it?" I asked breathlessly.

"I shan't tell you."

"But why *not?*"

"Because someone I love would be hurt."

"You mean…whoever killed my aunt will get away with it?"

Her face changed. It looked tired suddenly, and whiter than usual, emphasizing the red gash of her lip-sticked mouth. "Get away with it?" she repeated. "Well, in that sense, yes. But—"

She kneaded her furrowed brow with gnarled fingers. When she put her hands in her lap again her face was wry. "The things we do stay with us, you must know that. I still remember the way I castigated my little sister, who was my father's favorite. I was jealous, of course. I called her a fat pig, the worst thing I could think of, because she was so sensitive to being overweight. I sometimes wake at night and remember those cruel words, and the helpless tears that came to her eyes."

"But all the same, darling Elizabeth—"

"So you see," she said, interrupting, "living with guilt, day after day, is a horrible punishment. Worse than hanging. Oh yes. That person lives in a hell of their own making."

"Perhaps," I said. "But just the same I have some Calvinistic ideas about crime and punishment. I can't insist that you tell me who pushed that ladder, but I'll nag you about it. I'll ask you again. And again. I'll—"

"In the end," she said with a little smile, "you might feel the same as I. That when the time comes you won't do any more about it than I have. But it will be your decision."

"I don't know what you mean by that," I protested.

"Perhaps you never will," she said, stubbing out her cigarette,

I remembered the first evening I'd gotten to the Villa Paradiso. Elizabeth bending over the dead dog. *They're trying to frighten me…*

Was she afraid for her life? Had she meant the things she told me later had been said only in excitement and sorrow?

I leaned forward. "Why did Paolo die? You said someone was trying to frighten you. If you couldn't be seen by whoever pushed the ladder, why should that person have any reason to—"

"Because, my dear, that person realized almost *instantly* that I saw. Because that person knows I have damning evidence. Because in order to make sure that I'd keep quiet about it if I knew what was good for me, the only thing left I loved was put to death. Yes, Barbara, it was a warning, all right."

"But my aunt died several months ago, Elizabeth. Why was this warning just the other day? After all this time?"

"I can't answer that," she said, frowning.

"Maybe I can," I said slowly. "Signores Predelli and Pineider knew I was coming to Italy. More than likely, they mentioned it to the Monteverdis. And then, knowing a blood relative of Mercedes was to appear on the scene, they worried that you'd confide in me. And took steps."

"Why do you say the Monteverdis?" she asked.

"Why? Who else is there?"

"Lucrezia, Pietro, Emilio, lots of others."

"Oh no," I said surely. "You're talking about one of the family next door. You may be secretive about it, but you can't fool me all the way. You've told me a few things, now I'll tell *you* a few."

And I briefed her on the rat biscuits and the stained handkerchief that had belonged to my aunt. "Peter found out that it was your blood type," I said. "And so, of course, we both…well, wondered about it."

"I see," Elizabeth said. "Now I see everything. Oh, how awful, how terrible." She put a hand to her face, and I saw the fear in her eyes.

"How *awful*," she said again, and looked up quickly. "Barbara, go home. Go home. I mean it. It has nothing to do with you. Lucrezia will help you pack. Go to Rome…or Naples…but leave. Because—"

"Someone else told me to do that," I said. "But I'm not that kind of quitter. Why should I leave now? What have I done? Who has anything against me? Elizabeth, I'm staying."

The anger and the fury swept over me. What kind of nonsense was this? Be afraid of nameless terrors? Go home, tail between my legs, and…

"I'm not leaving," I said, with finality. "*Capisco?* I'm staying on until my holiday is up. I want to spend as much time as possible in my aunt's villa. And I've grown fond of her friend. I won't leave until it's time for me to go. And now, if you don't mind, I'd like a good stiff drink. I'm going to mix a batch of martinis. We're going to get a little bit sozzled. How about it, *cara?*"

"I think it sounds splendid," she said tremulously, and I saw her relieved eyes, that I was not going to leave her…not just yet.

I strode across the grass, adrenalin flowing through my veins. So they think they'll get the best of us, I was saying to myself. Damn them, damn them…

We'll just see about that, I decided, pouring gin into a pitcher with a heavy hand.

We would just see about *that*.

• • •

We had a delightful evening. The television was, as always, unreliable, with ghosts, snow and a garbled audio. We gave it up as a bad job and played scrabble. Elizabeth knew words I'd never heard of, British words. "Just a cotton picking *minute*," I kept saying, teasing her, and consulted the dictionary. But she was right "Natter" meant to speak garrulously, "hame" was a part of a harness.

"All right, if you want to cheat that way," I complained, and she laughed delightedly. "I do *so* enjoy your company," she cried, and before we went to bed, broke open a split of champagne from the refrigerator, over which we sat talking about our lives. "Men?

They're around, but no one I've fallen flat on my face for," I said, when she queried me, and she told me about her late husband. "A dear soul, but frightfully *impractical*," she assured me. "He left me with debts and that's about all, save for a broken heart. He was the only man I ever cared a fig about. Such an old dear, and I've never stopped missing him."

I smoked a last cigarette before going to bed in my room, brushed my teeth and then my hair, and got into bed. The soft breezes that drifted in through the opened french windows were like fingers stroking my skin. I was a bit stewed and nicely floating. America seemed like another planet, another life. As had Elizabeth Barrett, the poetess, I whispered to myself as I lay on my plump pillows, "Italy, Italy, Italy…"

The minute sounds of night insects soothed and comforted me. Little, living things strafing their tiny feet together. I was in love with life in all its forms, bewitched by nature and its magic. How beautiful, I thought falling asleep, was life.

•••

I woke with a smile on my face, watching the progress of the sun. First tinging the bureau with gold, then the table between the windows, and at last making a resplendent tracery of the patterns of the carpet. "Come and kiss me awake," I said to the sun, and it soon flooded over my bed and caressed my face with its fire.

I turned over in the bed, stretching, and when the knock came at my door, called out sleepily, "Okay, I'm awake, come in."

The door opened and Lucrezia was there.

"*Buon giorno,*" I said, smiling up at her. "*Come sta,* darling?"

And then I saw her face.

"What?" I asked, lifting my head from the pillows. "What's wrong, Lucrezia?"

"It's the signora," she said quietly. "I think she's dead."

Chapter Thirteen

She was undeniably dead. I knew right away that there was no life in that still body. Her face was as white as the cliffs of Dover. Her mouth, opened, was ghastly…her eyes were not quite closed, either. There was a flick of spittle at the corners of her lips.

"I found this," Lucrezia said, handing me a vial.

"Where?"

"On the table by the bed."

It was empty. Lucrezia said, "There were many, many pills in there. Sleeping pills, signorina."

"Yes I know."

I recognized the bottle. The red and green capsules I had brought to her, only the other night. At that time there must have been fifty or sixty capsules in the bottle. It was empty now, the lid off. And the woman in the bed was as white as a fish.

Lucrezia looked up at me. Her face crumpled. "The poor darling," she said, weeping. "She was lonely, *capisco?* Despondent. Oh, the poor signora…"

•••

The house was suddenly filled with people, both the lawyers, Predelli and Pineider, and Peter Fox, whom I had called at his hotel. The coroner was there, and Elizabeth Wadley was carted off to, I supposed, the local morgue. Or a funeral parlor. I had no rights in the matter and, furthermore, was functioning poorly. For the first time in my life events seemed to be sweeping so rapidly beyond me that I had lost control. "What are they going to do with her?" I remember asking Peter, to which he answered, "All in good time. I've called a doctor for you. I want you to have a sedative."

"Put me to sleep?" I demanded furiously. "And then what? They come and kill me too?"

"What do you mean by that?" he asked, his eyes probing mine.

"I saw the dust marks! Fingers prying! And the dog with blood on his muzzle…oh, you're not fooling me, Peter, any of you! A handkerchief drenched with blood…are you crazy? Or do you think *I* am? She was despondent, crying her eyes out for Mercedes? Fiddlesticks! She was just starting to live! First you say you're concerned about "dark events" and then you want to put me to sleep…and then they come in and leave marks in the dust and creep up to my bed and put a pillow over my head. Is *that* what you want? Can't you see the whole thing is insane? She didn't kill herself! I tell you, she—"

"What makes you question it?" he asked, smoothing back my hair.

"I just know it, I just know it. She didn't take the pills. Someone *made* her take them."

"Barbara," he said, kneading his fingers at the back of my neck. "God, you're uptight Just relax. Doesn't this feel good?"

"Yes, keep on doing it," I muttered.

He did, and after a while, when he had made me drink some brandy, and waited until I had dressed, he took me down the hill to lunch, at Doner's. My eyes were swollen and red and I kept my sunglasses on, but I was able to eat a little something and afterwards he took me for a long drive, through the Tuscan countryside.

We visited two estates of the *campagna*, cracked walnuts as big as hen's eggs, drank the *vino* of the region and, at a little before five, had cognac on a rooftop garden. I said I was terribly tired, that I didn't want dinner, but he was adamant. He insisted on a drink and a meal at the Trattoria Camillo in the old Medici Palace. He was a very comforting person and I wished I could feel more for him as a man. Here I was, at war, in my mind, with the Monteverdis, and all I could think of was dark-eyed Gianni.

I must be crazy…or sick, I thought. Why couldn't I forget about Gianni and think instead of Peter, this kind, wonderful man, who was being so *good* to me…

At shortly after ten he drove me back to the villa, which was blazing with lights on our side because, before I had left, I had asked Lucrezia to turn them all on, so that I wouldn't come home to darkness. That dear woman, in consideration of my plight, had agreed to stay the night away from her family to be with me. I couldn't have beared to be alone, and she knew it, had even offered her services before I asked.

Peter and I had a last cognac before he left, and it was agreed that he would phone me in the morning. "With whatever news I have about Elizabeth," he said, as if she were a living person and he was waiting to hear her pleasure. And then he went off; I heard the chug of the car outside, and the wheels scraping across the gravel. I passed Elizabeth's room, where Lucrezia was sleeping. There was a faint snoring, and nothing had ever sounded so good to me, that she was there, that I was not alone.

I went to my own room and made my preparations for bed. It came over me in waves, the tragedy, that Elizabeth was dead: I thought, no, it isn't possible and, brushing my teeth, fought tears. Oh, how awful, how awful, my mind, going round and round, kept repeating.

Oh, how awful…

• • •

Peter called at a few minutes before eight. Lucrezia roused me. "It is signore Fox," she said, and I got out of bed and went to the phone.

"Yes, Peter," I said.

"You're okay?"

"Yes, I'm okay."

"When are you leaving?"

"Today. Or tomorrow."

"Today," he said.

"Probably."

"I'll call for you."

"No, don't. I'll take my time packing and get a taxi. I'll go back to the Continentale. I imagine they'll be able to accomodate me."

"I'll call them and let you know. All right?"

"Yes, thanks very much."

The lawyers showed up again just after I had finished showering and dressing. Signore Pineider had a quiet conversation with Lucrezia, while Signore Predelli took me aside. After asking how I was feeling, he said he had something for me.

"For me?" I asked, dully. I couldn't imagine what he meant.

"Mrs. Wadley gave it to us, to my partner and me," he said. "She told us it was to be opened only in the event of her death. Which was what started us thinking, because her behavior was so singular. She said a few things, equivocal things, that made us wonder about the death of the Contessa, your aunt. We first put it down to hysteria and grief. But in the light of certain other matters—"

He lifted his eyebrows. "Well, as time went on," he continued, "both Arturo and I had second thoughts. That perhaps the signora Wadley knew something of grave import. That there was indeed an aspect to your aunt's death which—"

He became brusque. "But it is now all in the past," he said, and I saw that he was not unaffected by Elizabeth's death. He took out a handkerchief and blew his nose loudly. Then he reached in another pocket and pulled out a small package.

"Signorina, she gave us this envelope, but a few days after you were here she called and said that she had changed her mind. That if something were to happen to her we were to give this to you. That it would be your decision."

He handed it to me.

It was a manila envelope, about four by six, sealed. I took it, wonderingly, and in my mind his words echoed. I remembered someone else saying, *"It will be your decision…"*

Elizabeth had said those words to me. Under the trees, in the garden, just yesterday. And then, *"When the time comes you might not do any more about it than I have."*

I turned the package over in my hands. Something rattled inside. "But what is this?" I asked signore Predelli.

"I haven't the faintest idea," he said. "And it no longer has anything to do with me, signorina. It is in your hands now."

He smiled gravely, adding, "I have done what was asked of me. I hope you know, my dear young lady, that whatever my partner and I can do, in your behalf, we will gladly do, and most humbly. You have had a rough time of it. I hope you can put it behind you, and remember only the good things about our country. There was a smile on your face the first day I met you. Before you leave Italy, I hope the smile will return to your lovely eyes."

"I hope so," I said mechanically, and then Eleanora skipped into the room, coming from the garden through the french doors. She smiled, dimples appearing, and started babbling.

"Nonna saw the car," she said. "She told me, tell them to come over for coffee. *Si?*"

She stood on one leg.

"She waits for you. *Prego?*"

"Ah, certainly," Signore Pineider said, kissing the tips of the child's fingers. "We can surely spare a moment to say hello to the Signora Monteverdi."

"And you too, signorina," Eleanora said to me. "*P'cere?* You come too, please?"

"Darling, I can't just—"

She seized my hand. "You come too," she said, pleading. "You know, signorina, I saw some cakes, with frosting. *Bella, bella.* Good to eat. Beautiful. So if you please, signorina."

Signores Predelli and Pineider laughed. "Who could refuse such an invitation," Pineider said, a cigarette dangling from his lips. And as we walked into the sunlight, making our way across the grass to the adjoining gate, both men inhaled deeply. "A fine property," Signore Predelli said, glancing round appreciatively. "One of the best in Florence. I understand that Bernard Berenson called it La Divina Terra. And yes, it is all of that."

We had strong coffee and some little iced cakes, served by the Principessa, in the living room of the Monteverdi's part of the house. I saw at once that the room was much like that of my aunt's, with vaulted ceiling, open hearth and mullioned windows. Francesca was there, and the Principe, and it was quiet and civilized. Eleanora gobbled up three sweet cakes and then reached for my hand.

"Signorina, I would show you my room," she said.

The adults laughed, as the child tugged at my arm. I felt awkward, but the Principessa graciously indicated that I might take my leave. Francesca said she hoped her daughter's room was not too disarranged. "Children, you understand. Please take into consideration—"

"Come," Eleanora said impatiently. "And you can see my puppets. A monkey and a Punchinello. Also, I have a tiger."

"Excuse me," I said to the others. "*Buon giorno*, Signore Predelli, Signore Pineider."

"Come come," the child exhorted.

"Yes, darling." I was carted off, but before leaving, said to Signore Predelli, "About the package Mrs. Wadley left for me, thank you for it. I knew her for only a few short days, but she had become a cherished friend. To have something belonging to her makes me happy. Thanks again, and I'll certainly be in touch with you before I leave for home."

Signore Predelli was brusque. "Yes, signorina," he said. *Arrivaderci, signorina. Buona fortuna.*"

"Thank you," I said, and we climbed the stairs to the upper story. It was the first time I had thought about it, but now I reflected that it was strange, the Monteverdis having the lion's share of the villa. My aunt's part of it was one-storied, with only two bedrooms and two baths, but this half of the property had two floors. And then I remembered that Mercedes and her husband had been barren, whereas the Principessa, fecund, had borne children. Mercedes hadn't needed the extra rooms: she had lived, as on an island, with her beloved, in the smaller part of the house. And had evidently been happy there, with her adored Conte.

"I wish I could have known her," I said aloud.

"*Per favore?*" Eleanora asked.

"Just thinking," I said, and then we came to her room. It was the usual child's chamber, with Mother Goose wallpaper and a youth bed, a small armoire and a *semainier*. She pulled open drawers and regaled me with glimpses of gauzy nightgowns and tiny little panties, opened the wardrobe and pointed out dresses and chic little pants suits.

"Oh, how nice, Eleanora."

She manipulated her puppets, little bits of cloth in the shapes of apes, tigers and puppies. "Grr," she cried, thrusting her hands into a cross-eyed animal, and laughed as I pretended to be frightened.

At last I said I must be running along.

"Very well," she said graciously, and took my hand as we left her child's room. In the hall she pointed. "That's Mama and Papa's room. You want to see it?"

She insisted. "Come, I show you."

She guided me inside Francesca and Benedetto's room. It was lovely, a suite really, with bedchamber, sitting room and bath. "Papa sleeps here," she said, indicating the outside of the double bed.

"Oh."

"And Mama sometimes sleeps there."

She pointed to a chaise longue on the other side of the room. "When they are angry," she said gravely.

"Oh?" Out of the mouths of babes, I thought, and her hand drew me on. "Now this is Gianni's room. My dear Gianni. It's small, *si?* But he doesn't mind."

She stood, just inside the doorway, on one leg. "I like this room," she said "It has the most sun. See his bed? It is almost like mine."

And indeed it was narrow, almost like that of a monk. Eleanora stroked the bedcover. "My Gianni," she said softly. "I love him so much. This is not a very big room, is it? But he is happy here, he told me so. He said, "Nora, this is my castle. A castle, signorina? What does that mean?"

"It means a whole private life," I said gently. "It means something of your own. If Gianni feels that way about this little room, we can both envy him. He's lucky, can you understand that? That Gianni doesn't need estate or title?"

She looked into my face. "I don't know what that means, estate or title," she said gravely.

"Some day you will," I said, putting my arms around her. "I only hope not too soon. Just be a little girl for as long as you can. Darling, you're so sweet."

I bent and kissed her. She *was* sweet. She smelt of flowers, or the warm, innocent fragrance of childhood. "And this is Nonna and Nonno's room," she said, leading me on, preceding me into still another bedchamber. Like her mother's and father's, it was a suite, with sitting room, bedroom and bath. The sitting room overlooked the gardens.

"See," she said. "Nonno reads his paper here." She walked over to the window. "Sometimes he falls asleep. I come in and go over to him and he wakes up. Then he sits me on his lap and we look out the window." She giggled. "He likes to watch Pietro working, with Emilio. "Get to work, I'm watching you," he calls down, "*Pigro imbecilles…*" And they look up and laugh."

Mentally, I translated. *You lazy bums…*

Eleanora's face became grave suddenly. She pointed. "It was there, you see, where the signora was on the ladder."

She put out a hand, her face wistful. "I wish she was there now, signorina. I would reach out and touch her. I would say, 'Hey, signora, get to work.'"

She leaned on the window sill, her face on a plump little arm. Her eyes were thoughtful, and remembering. I looked at her and, after a while said, puzzled, "What do you mean, Eleanora? The signora? There? I thought she was…I mean, wasn't she in her own garden? On the other side?"

"No, right there," she said pensively. "I could touch her now, if she…."

Her eyes had a faraway look. "You know, she had funny hair, like—"

She made little squiggles with her hands.

"Curly?"

"*Si.* My fingers would get all tangled."

I sat there and thought of what Peter had said. "The ladder, think of the ladder…"

And now I thought of the ladder, my ideas rearranging slowly. Not in the other garden, but in this one, so near to this window, where the Principe sat, that one could reach out and touch Mercedes's hair, her face…

Or do something else…

A vivid, terrible picture sprang into my mind. The Principe sitting here at the window, reading his newspaper. Mercedes up on the ladder, only a hand-span away. He sat looking at her, thinking of his son's gambling debts. Not only about the gambling debts. About his lost property. About his lost sovereignty. All this had once been his…and was his no longer. And the woman on the ladder, trimming away parasite vines…so near to him, so near…

He looked out, meeting her eyes.

And then, in a flash, put out a hand.

Mercedes, her own eyes unbelieving, widening.

And then her indrawn breath, as the hand touched the ladder. The ladder swaying, the vines brushing her face…

I felt dizzy, and sat down quickly in the chair by the window.

And at last I was sure. That was the way it had happened. Of course, I thought. Of course.

And that man knowing, almost instantly, that he had been seen, when Elizabeth dashed across the lawn, plunging through the gate. He knew he had been spotted. And had lived in terror ever since. Such terror that he had poisoned the little dog, in a last ditch effort to cover his traces, to frighten Elizabeth into silence.

"Do you have a headache, like Papa?" Eleanora asked, looking concerned.

"No, it's just the heat. It's a hot day, isn't it?"

"I don't mind it."

"Let's go down now. I have things to attend to."

"Where is the signora?"

"I haven't been told yet."

"She's dead too, isn't she?"

"Yes, but you see, darling, she was old, perhaps she wouldn't mind. At any rate, you're not to think about it"

"No, and I shan't grieve. Mama told me so."

"That's right. What's done is done." We went down the stairs together. The lawyers had left, and I made my way over to the other garden. Emilio, the son of Pietro the gardener, was weeding around some bushes. He looked up shyly as I started to pass him, and said, *"Buon giorno."*

On an impulse I stopped. "Where's your father?" I asked.

"Not feeling well today," he said, in labored English. "Couldn't come."

I stood beside him. "I'm leaving the villa," I told him.

He ducked his head and murmured something. I didn't quite catch it, but assumed he was telling me he was sorry. I said, "Yes, so am I. It turned out so badly."

"*Si,*" he said, shaking his head. "*Male, male.*"

"Now you'll be working for the Monteverdis."

He shrugged. Work…he had to work. What did it matter whom he worked *for?*

I said, "Emilio, when my aunt died, the Contessa, you were here, weren't you?"

"*Si.*"

"The ladder was near the other house?"

"*Si,* signorina."

"And the little girl was standing beside it?"

"Oh, no," he said. "The little girl was at the upstairs window."

I stared at him. "What do you mean? The signora had asked her to fetch some shears."

"Yes," he said. "She looked in the window and asked the little girl to go down for the shears. And then the child did, so after that she was upstairs again. I was working, and my father too, and then there was a terrible scream. The signora, you understand. My father ran, and I too, but it was too late."

He made a sound between his teeth. "She was dead, the signora."

He sighed. "And then they were all there. It was…I will never forget it."

"I can certainly understand that," I said. "Emilio, when the signora, my aunt, fell to her death, where were the others?"

He looked at me, questioning. "*Per favore?*" he asked, not quite understanding.

I was trying to set the scene, for the last and final time, in my mind. I said, "For example, where was Mrs. Wadley?"

"She was there," he said, pointing to the garden table.

"And you and your father?"

"Over there." He indicated a spot not far from where we were.

"And who was in the other garden? The Monteverdis' garden?"

"No one was there," he said. "Only when the accident occurred. They ran out of the house."

"But when she was on the ladder, there was no one in the garden next door?"

"Only the signora," he said. "On the ladder."

"One more thing, Emilio. Do you have rats here?"

His eyes, astonished, looked into mine.

"Rats?"

"I mean…are there rats hereabouts?"

"But no," he said, astounded. "Rats? Never, signorina. Maybe near the river, *posso*. But never up here. Sometimes field mice, *piccolo*, but never rats."

"Thank you, Emilio," I said. "I know you and your father must have wages coming to you. I'll see what I can do about it. You won't be cheated."

"*Grave.*"

"*Buona fortuna*, Emilio."

"*Buona fortuna*, signorina," he answered and, with his shy eyes looking away quickly, bent to his weeding again.

•••

I went into the house and, closing the door of my room, opened the package Elizabeth had left for me. As soon as I slit it open I knew why it had rattled. There were two things in there, both gold. One was a handsome watch which, when I looked closely at it, bore the engraved initials of the Principe on its back. I didn't know his first or middle name, but the last letter, elaborately curli-cued, was an M.

"You won't find your watch," the Principessa had said to her husband, on my first morning at the villa.

"No, I am afraid it is gone forever…"

I put it down on the bed and looked at the other gold object. Delicate, dainty, fit for a small, childish neck…a heart-shaped locket on a slender chain.

And that was all.

I thought about it for a long, long time. Held both golden objects in my hands. And now I knew who had killed Mercedes. Or at least knew that one of them had. There had been a woman on a ladder, perhaps chatting gaily with the two persons inside the window just beyond. An old man and a little girl. And then, while she scarcely credited the evidence of her own eyes, someone had leaned out and pushed her, sent her hurtling to her death.

Reaching out, in desperation, unbelieving, her hands had seized a gold watch and a gold locket. First thin air, as she tried to steady herself and then, perhaps sobbing frantically, her grasping fingers had clutched, as if at life, whatever they came in contact with.

A man's watch and a child's locket.

But who had done the pushing?

The Principe? It seemed logical. Proud, deprived, emasculated…despising the woman who had disinherited him. Yes, I could picture him, in that one lightning moment, putting his hand out and —

But the child had been there too, according to Emilio. It had been from *that* vantage point that Mercedes had asked for the shears, and the child had gotten them. And then had gone upstairs again.

And the other picture came into my mind. The little hand going out, perhaps even in a spirit of fun…to touch the curly, gray hair of an old woman and then, mischievous, not knowing what she was doing, gave a shove…

Or knowing what she was doing…

I had the watch and the locket. Signifying nothing. Elizabeth had seen, but I hadn't. And I would never know. Peter had questions, and the signores Predelli and Pineider had questions. Only Elizabeth had known what hand had sent my aunt to her death…and Elizabeth was dead too.

I remembered her words. *It will be your decision…*

I sat there until the bright day faded into dusk. I kept thinking about that beautiful, tawny-haired little girl, and hoped, against hope, that hers hadn't been the hand that had left Mercedes, her neck broken, dead on the grass. I kept thinking that she had remembered me, whom she had never seen, and thought of me as "little Barbara," in the same way she had almost certainly thought of the child next door as "little Eleanora." That, perhaps because of Eleanora, she had recalled a child of her own flesh and blood, however far removed, and so had made me a legatee in her will. If she had loved that child next door, desired her as she would have desired a daughter of her own, what were her last thoughts…if Eleanora had put out that fatal hand and sent the ladder flying?

I didn't want to dwell on it. My heart was heavy and I thought of Elizabeth, lying who knew where. Elizabeth, who in a few short days, had come to be my friend. Mercedes was an X quantity: I would never know what she was *really* like, but I had known her friend and companion and had, perhaps, come to love her.

I went out to the garden and looked down into the valley.

Down there lay a city I had begun to cherish, a city to which, perhaps, I had come home. Someone of my own blood had passionately adored that city, and the Italian ethos, and the stones that had been there for centuries. There was no possible way that Mercedes could have guessed that a girl from America would sigh and muse, as she herself had, over the glory she had found and never left. She had met a young man and woman, newly-married, had liked them, had enjoyed their company so much that their shapshot, in a gilt frame, was among countless others on the silk scarf that covered the top of the Boesendorfer grand. She might have forgotten them, in the welter of her rich life, but some stray cell in her brain, toward the end of her life, brought them to mind again, and she remembered that they had a child, as she had not, a child named Barbara.

I knew then that Elizabeth had been right, that I would never say anything. For there would be no advantage. Elizabeth had told me, when explaining why she kept her knowledge to herself, "It would hurt someone I love."

I thought, she meant Gianni. I knew she had cared deeply for that Italian boy. And I knew that Gianni meant something quite important to me as well. I couldn't hurt him. But it was more than that. History is made of small crimes and large ones, small greatnesses and large ones, and in the end the final arbiter is what some call God but is really the hidden writing on the unseen wall. We live with secrets, all of us, even as that beautiful child Eleanora, in our jealously-guarded wicker baskets, and the sum of every man's life is known only to himself. We die with our pitiful misdeeds buried in our stilled hearts.

I sealed the package again, put it into my suitcase and then, remembering the dust marks of a few days ago, took it out again. No, I thought, no. Because it had suddenly come to me that *someone* next door knew of the missing items, and the terrible meaning of them...I didn't dare leave that package about, for someone to find. I couldn't chance it.

I peeped out of my room, didn't see Lucrezia, and with the package under my sweater, went into the vaulted drawing room. There was a little niche, behind a bust of Dante, and I crept across the room and hid the package there. It was high up, so high that I had to stand on a chair, and I doubted that Lucrezia would cover that particular spot in a day's dusting, especially under the sad circumstances.

It was completely hidden and I felt it was well done, that telltale package far from the sight of prying eyes. I went back to my room and, not knowing what provisions had been made for Lucrezia, made up my mind that I would tell her that she would be repaid, by myself, for her time and services, that when I came into my inheritance, I would share some of it with her. Because she had been so kind to me. I felt like giving it all away; it didn't mean anything to me any longer.

She made a luscious supper, and we ate in the garden, early, because she couldn't take another night off. She had a husband and children; she had a life. "You'll be all right?" she asked, when she had washed up the dishes and was ready to leave.

"Of course," I said, and watched her rush off on her Vespa, vanishing down the steep road. I went into the house again, all alone, leaving a trail of lights behind me as I went to my room. Peter Fox had called, saying that the Hotel Continentale had a room for me. He had wanted to take me there immediately, but I said no, just one more night at the Villa Paradiso, because after all it belonged to someone else now, and I would never set foot on it again, ever.

He seemed to understand, said he would be there if I wanted to call him. But I didn't want to call him. I lay in bed for a long time, listening to the night sounds, and wanted to cry. But I couldn't. Finally I got up, took two aspirins, and went back to bed. In the morning Lucrezia would be there, would wake me up with ineffable smells…bacon sizzling, and eggs done to a turn. I didn't lie in darkness; I couldn't bear to. I left a small light burning on the writing table near the windows. Weary, doleful, I closed my eyes and, sighing, fell asleep. A soft breeze drifted in from the outdoors. The sheets were cool, and felt so good, so good…

Chapter Fourteen

My eyes opened. I lay stiffly, retreating from some dream or other. There was something my mind was trying to tell me. For a moment, I tried to recapture the dream…there had been a child, and the child had smiled up at me. But, frowning, I admitted to my waking self that the smile had been strange…and *not* child-like…but curiously adult.

Oh, I was dreaming about Eleanora, I thought, as I came out of my night stupor. What a funny smile she wore…not very nice, not at all nice…

I was by then fully awake.

Weirdly awake. There was a notion in my mind. There was something, something…

I plumped my pillows and pondered. Yes, there was something… something that bothered me.

Something nagging at me…

The lamp, whose shade I had tipped, made a warm arc, golden and comforting. I burrowed into the pillows and asked myself what it was that tried to pierce my consciousness.

And then, in a flash, I knew.

Elizabeth, in her bed, white as a ghost and dead as a doornail… from an overdose of sleeping pills.

But lying on her right side…

On her righi side…

It was all, suddenly, as clear as a bell. Of course, I thought, of course. Lying on her right side…the "bad" side. When she woke in the night, having turned, in her sopor, to that poor, crippled hip, she'd screamed. Had waked me. Screamed out in pain…and I'd rushed in to her.

Then how could it be, I asked myself, that, having taken an overdose, "despondent at having lost her lifelong friend, the

Contessa," she had swallowed the pills and settled in the bed on her right side…which meant agony for her…meant pain that brought her awake, screaming…

No, I thought. No. If she took the overdose, depressed, finally wanting to end her life, she would turn to her "good" side, perhaps say something to God, or whomever she believed in, and drift off…forever…

But she certainly wouldn't…couldn't…do it on her crippled side.

I was cold, and shivering. I knew it, I told myself. I knew it. Someone pushed the pills down her throat. Someone forced them into her mouth.

Someone…

I knew it all along, I said aloud, talking to myself. I knew it. There was a dark story, yes. About Mercedes, my aunt, the late Contessa, and about her "beloved enemy," Elizabeth Wadley. Both of them. Both of them had been put to death. A Monteverdi had done it. A member of that disinherited family had done it. Killed two women, one after the other, so that the Villa Paradiso would revert to the original owners. Cruelly, with malice aforethought, one of them had slain first my aunt, then the dog, and then Elizabeth.

I must call Peter in the morning, I thought, and checked my bedside clock to set the alarm for seven. And then I turned over again, my head heavy and aching dully, pulling up the sheet to cover the glare of the lamp. I was so tired I could have cried. It had been an ordeal, and to be up to it, to get the best of it, I needed a few hours respite.

And then I fell asleep.

• • •

I woke because my hand was asleep. Ugh, I thought dimly, and started chopping away at it, not fully alert, but trying to bring the blood back to my numbed member. It felt like a lump of clay. I wrung it, trying to flex the fingers.

I was, suddenly, wide awake.

The light was out. The lamp near the windows, which I had left burning, was burning no longer.

Why, I wondered, stiffening. Why?

I lay in the darkness, my heart hammering.

Why was the light out?

I heard the furtive steps. Tensed, listening, every nerve taut. God, I thought. I was in the dark…*and someone was in this room…*

For a minute or two longer I lay there, cravenly, trying not to gasp, or show that I was awake. And then, gathering my forces together, while the faint light of the half moon, raying in from outdoors, showed me the dark shadow a few steps away, I drew my legs up, as silently as possible, pushed the covers back and then, with a gargantuan effort, jumped out of bed. Barefoot, I plunged toward the open windows, stifling a scream, and in the next moment was tearing across the wet grass, my breath sobbing in my throat.

Reason made me opt for the dividing gate between the division of the villa. Because there were people there. One of them might be intent on my destruction, but the others, sleeping above, would come to my aid. I zigzagged crazily, my feet drenched with the night dew and, about to screech my lungs out, found a hand over my mouth. I froze, as if ice had formed over my heart. I was still, for seconds, feeling the cold grip of death on me, unable to move a muscle.

And then I found a sudden, superhuman strength. I writhed, trying to release myself, while the hands wound tighter around me.

"Let me go," I sobbed, wrenching at them.

"Please…*per favore*…please…"

I knew Gianni's voice.

"It's me," he said. "It's me."

I wrenched a hand free, drove at him, hissing like a snake. I felt like an animal at bay. *"Let me go…"*

A mouth came down over mine, crashing, with opened lips, against mine. My hands scrabbled up and down, against him, trying to push him away, trying, desperately, to get free of him.

"Let me go, let me go!"

His lips left mine. With strong hands he imprisoned me. I could feel his heart beating. "No," he said. "No. Listen to me, *listen to me.*" He bent back one of my wrists; the pain was almost unbearable. I felt the water come into my mouth, and the tears smarted my eyes.

"Please don't," I whispered. "Don't hurt me."

"Then you must be quiet," he said inexorably.

"Yes, I will…but please don't hurt me like that…"

His voice was rough. "I only want to love you," he said harshly, and his mouth came down again, mashing against mine. And against all reason, with my heart beating wildly against the cage of my chest, I returned his kiss. Wound my arms around his neck. I must be utterly crazy, I thought in a daze. Crazy…

At last I broke free, whispered, pleasing. "What?" I asked. "What do you want? Please, Gianni, let me go. Please."

He released me. "You won't scream?" he asked anxiously.

I stood trembling. "No, I won't scream. But what is it? Why did you come into my room? Don't you understand how frightening it was? I'm all alone. And then the light was out…"

I felt a hand, soft, in my hair. "I didn't want to frighten you," he said, and his voice was like a caress. "I'm so sorry, darling."

"Well, you nearly drove me out of my mind," I said, tearfully. "How could you *do* that?"

"Please forgive me. I just wanted to talk to you. I *must* talk to you. There are things I must know."

"What?" I cried, and shivered in the cool night. It was, after all, almost October, and I wore only a nightgown. I was half out of my mind. The light out…and standing here in the damp grass…

"It's about the package," he said.

"What package?" I snapped it out like a drill sergeant.

"The one Predelli gave you. From the signora Wadley."

"What about it?"

"Because," he said, "my mother and father were upset. It had something to do with that, the package."

He grasped my arm. "What was it?"

"None of your business," I said, angrily.

"It is my business," he said quietly. "Yes. Because I know there is something wrong. Crazy thoughts? Possibly. I am sensitive to emotions, to faces, particularly those of my own family. Listen, I saw them, my mother and father, when you said to signore Predelli about the package from the signora. You understand? But no, how could you? My father is a child. My mother his mother. Yes, she loves her sons, I am sure, but she adores Papa, she worries so about him. Not really about Benedetto, who lives a truly dangerous life. Me? In her mind I am like little Eleanora. A boy, a child. Just that, no more. But my father—"

He held my hand, but not brutally, and I felt his breath on my cheek. "Barbara, listen," he said. "I could see that she was very concerned about him, right after the lawyers left. They went upstairs, and were there all of the day. Now you must tell me what it means."

"I can't."

"But you *must*."

"I'm sorry. I can't. It's their life. Just let it go. It doesn't concern you."

"If it concerns you, then it concerns me," he said, "that package, I want to know what it was."

"I can't tell you."

"But why, but why?"

"Because I can't."

"I don't understand," he said, passionately. "You put your mouth against mine…your arms around me…and then refuse to—"

"Will you leave me *alone?*"

I pounded at him. "Leave me alone!"

And then I screamed it.

"Leave me alone, let me go!"

A light sprang on, up above. Someone said, thickly, *"Che cosa?"*

And then another light lit the darkness.

"Now you see what you've done," I said shakily. "Now they're awake…now are you satisfied?"

His arms fell away. His voice, almost a whisper, sounded defeated. "So go," he said, low. "Then go. I thought—"

"I don't know what you thought, but look what you've done! They've heard us…can't you see it won't do any good?"

I sprang away, raced across the sodden grass, gained my room again. My God, I thought, my God. In the middle of the night… in the middle of the night…

I turned on the lamp again, sat on the edge of my bed and, laying a finger across my lips, remembered. I'm terribly in love with him, I whimpered to myself. I'm so terribly in love with Gianni. But how could he have frightened me like that?

I jumped up and started packing. Frantically, I threw garments into my suitcase. Trembling, I stuffed cosmetics into my Elizabeth Arden valise. *Ave*, I thought, mumbling it to myself. *Ave atque vale.* My Aunt Mercedes had been luckier. She had found peace and beauty here.

I had found sadness, terror, cruelty, and a phantasmagoria of riddles. There would be no smile on my face when I left the Villa Paradiso. I was a whipped dog.

How horribly it had turned out…

Chapter Fifteen

Peter called in the morning.

"Are you packed?"

"Yes, everything's done."

"I'll pick you up at around noon."

"Please don't. I'll call a taxi."

"But why? I want to—"

"Don't press it," I said. "I'm going by taxi. If you don't mind, Peter."

"Whatever you say," he answered, and rang off.

And I didn't leave. I stayed there the whole day, looking at the photographs on the Boesendorfer, wandering through the empty rooms, sitting in the garden, aching, aching, for what I was leaving behind. The hours went by and still I stayed, listening to the voices next door, at *aperitivi* time, and then through their dinner hour, with the laughter and the camaraderie and the family close, close… clannish, alien to me. Once, I thought, this property belonged to Mercedes, the late Contessa; it had been hers, she had loved and cherished it, and now it was theirs, the Monteverdis. I hated them, briefly, and when they went into the house, because of mosquitoes, told myself good riddance, and sat there in the silence.

I was only an intruder now.

I went inside again, got out the package with the watch and the locket. I knew what I was going to do with it. I was going to bury it. Beside Paolo. I thought it was fitting. I even said, as I held it in my hands, "La *commedia e finita*…"

And then I went out, in the cool of the evening, to the twisted pine tree. I felt very lonely. It was the last dusky evening I would spend here. I had gone to the shed, in the courtyard, for a spade, and I walked across the grass to the dwarfed tree.

I knelt on the ground, which was a little damp and, turning over the earth with the spade, I dug a hole. The rich soil, yielding a few startled worms, sifted through my fingers. When the hole was deep enough, I pulled the watch and the locket out of my pocket. I held them for a moment. Ten years from now, perhaps a hundred, these trinkets might be found.

Blinded suddenly by tears, because it had turned out in this unexpected, sad way, I fondled the watch, crushed the tiny locket to my breast, and because of the tears did not see the figure that stood beside me. "In a permanent dark dream of a forest of firs," I was thinking, bereft and lonely with no one to witness this final, inexorable act, I almost lost my balance when I heard the voice.

"Signorina," someone said, and almost at once, as I blinked rapidly, I knew that voice.

"Principessa?" I asked, using the forbidden title, and looked up.

She was standing there, in half silhouette, framed by the house lights, the brilliant illumination from the valley below, and the half moon. She looked down at me, with a kind of stern curiosity and said, "What are you doing, signorina?"

I dropped the watch and locket, which I had slipped into its envelope again, into the hole.

"Something I have to do," I said.

"I want to know."

"It doesn't concern you," I said, and started to push back the earth to cover the envelope.

"I think it does."

"May I remind you that you're on my property," I said, trembling.

"No," she said. "Not your property. Mine. Ours."

She was suddenly on her knees beside me. I tried to stop her, but she pushed me aside. And then, scrabbling in the earth, she drew out the envelope. I did my best to take it away from her, but she was a strong woman, and she wrested my hands away. She ripped open the envelope, shaking the dust from it, and pulled out the watch and the heart-shaped locket Calmly, she examined both and looked long at the watch. Her face softened for a moment and then crumpled shockingly.

"So it's true," she whispered, and then turned to me.

"But my dear young woman," she said, as if she were talking to a child, to Eleanora. "Bury these if you will, but you would always know where they were. And some day, some time, you would tell someone."

"No," I said vehemently. "No, Principessa. Never. It would hurt someone I love."

She laughed, a bitter sound. "You love no one here," she said coldly. And, as with Lucia, the earthy expletive broke from her.

"*Mama mia*…you say love? You make me laugh, signorina. What do you know about love? You sicken me…"

Her voice was harsh now, chilling me. I felt she had become unmanageable, though I tried to reason with her. "Don't you see," I cried. "I was hiding these things! So that no one could—"

"But one day you will say to someone, "My aunt was murdered, and I have the proof." Her eyes were blazing in the dusky light, and she palmed the gold watch and locket. "Crucify us, you would do that, yes I know."

She scrambled up, glaring down at me. "Signorina, I am afraid not," she said menacingly. "And you too want to take what is ours away from us…you too, from foreign soil, want to torment us. That woman! All of you, you Americans, like locusts, like a plague…with your dollars…we hate you, don't you know that? All of us, we hate you!"

Her eyes were cold and terrible. I fell back. Such anger, such rage…what had I done, after all? I had fallen in love with her country, with her city, with her estate, her way of life, and with her son. And in my wild love affair with Italy, with Firenze, had tried to erase the traces of a murder…two murders. I wouldn't have harmed the Monteverdis…never, never. My intent had been only to cover up the bloody hands of those who had been responsible for Mercedes's death, and Elizabeth's death.

I had been a deliberate accessory to a crime…two crimes.

And she looked at me like that!

"I was in your room," she said quietly. "I see that your luggage is ready to go. Why don't you go, signorina?"

"That was my intention," I said and, backing up, was afraid. I didn't like the look in her eyes. The face, fine, and the product of a thousand years of Florentine civilization, was suddenly evil, cruel. The strong, gray-white hair, tidily piled into a chignon at the nape, seemed Medusa-like. The woman who confronted me was a woman I was afraid of.

"I'm going now," I said.

"You can take the car," she assured me, her lips curving into a strange smile. "After all, they're both dead, she and the Contessa. You might as well claim the car."

"I thought I'd call a taxi."

My lips were dry. I was *dying* to call a taxi, have a strong, experienced Italian driver help me get my bags into the back seat of his vehicle and take me away from the Villa Paradiso. Paradiso! Villa Infernale would be more to the point.

"That's ridiculous," she said briskly and, incredibly, smiled. "Let me help you with your luggage."

"I don't need help. Thank you, but—"

"I say again, you don't need a taxi," she replied and walked past me, striding over the grass, to the house. She disappeared inside it.

I panicked. Oh no, I thought. I won't let her get the best of me. Certainly not. I streaked over the grass and went round the house, scrabbling over the pebbles in the driveway. I came to the courtyard and the Principessa was coming out the front, with a bag under each arm. Over her shoulder was my cosmetic case, dangling loosely.

"Is there anything else?" she asked politely, as she dropped the bags to the ground.

"That's all, and thank you. Now I'll go in and call a taxi."

It was a pleasant, warm evening, but my teeth were chattering. I spoke between them, trying to discipline myself. "Thank you, signora."

Because her face was so strange. So determined. I was terrified at the look in her eyes. And when she picked up my bags again, opened the back seat of the Lancia and stowed them in, I wanted to scream. And I guess I did.

"I said I was going to call a taxi!"

"But you won't," she said grimly. "Get in."

She came toward me threateningly. *"I said get in."*

"No."

I saw the other car, already parked on the road. I saw that and then faced her again. My voice shook; I was ashamed of it, but my God, her infuriated eyes! She stood in my path, like a bull at a *corrida*, with the same inflamed eyes. This is terrible, I thought, this is terrible…and I tried to sidestep her. With that, a hand came out and whacked me in the face. Like a sledgehammer. A strong, brutal hand. It brought tears to my eyes and I ducked as the hand came toward me again.

"Get in the car," she said.

And now I knew. That there was no escape. If I didn't get in the car she would shove me in, whamming at me with that hard, pitiless hand. I was her prisoner. This woman planned my destruction and, by whatever means, was determined that I was to die. Like the others. She would silence me, to protect her family's interest, with whatever means possible. I would never live to tell the tale. I saw it in her hard, wicked, implicable face. That there would be no one left to reveal the terrible truth. I was to be the final victim.

I took one look at that cold and determined face and scrambled behind the wheel of the Lancia. Frantically, I started the motor. In the rear view mirror, as the car spurted forward, I saw the Principessa climbing into her own car. The dust churned up as my wheels circumnavigated the turn of the driveway, and then I was rocketing down that narrow, serpentine road, the spit of gravel pitting the metal of the car.

I should have let Peter come for me, I thought, stepping on the gas. The other car, behind me, screamed with a shriek of the tires, and I saw it in the oblong of the overhead mirror. What the hell was she doing? I asked myself, but knew. Why, she wanted to drive me off the road…

I knew what was in her mind, I knew. Please, I thought… others had died before me. My aunt, and then the little dog, and Elizabeth. It wasn't this madwoman who had brought about those other murders…but this madwoman would protect, perhaps with her life and at the cost of mine, the person who had done them. I was expendable too…and as I rounded a turn, knew it wouldn't even make headlines. An American girl had plunged to her death, at a break in the road, and cindered to her end.

And no one would be blamed.

It would be only a few lines at the bottom of a column. Of interest to no one. Just another tourist accident. But my life means more to me than that, my mind shrieked, as I came to one of those terrible, open places, where the valley below, thousands of feet down, was brilliantly lit, hospitable. I pressed down on the gas, standing on it, praying. The other car was so near, and that white, hideous face behind the wheel, the teeth drawing the lips back…if she sideswiped me now it would be the end. I would hurtle down, over and over, and would be shipped back to the United States in bits and pieces.

No, I thought wildly. No. I will not die like that. And realized that only a desperate measure on my part could save me. The brilliant lights of the other car blinded me, and breath rasped in my throat. I rounded another bend, the car zooming behind me like an implacable Nemesis, and I made up my mind. I stepped on the gas and—I think I was praying—drove into a plane tree at the side of the road. The tree loomed up at me and I said to myself, "God help me," and the car crashed into the tree. My car door opened and I flew into the air, my ears singing, and lay there, listening to an Italian song, a very beautiful one.

"Come back to Sorrento…"

Pain seared my body. I knew at once that one of my arms was broken, and then I saw the flames, as I blacked out. But not for long. I realized, almost instantly, that I was at the very edge of the road, and I was looking down at the lights below, in the valley. I saw the other car plunging over the cliff, like a toy, rolling over and over, and there was no sound, simply a hulk of metal leaving the road and plummeting down, down to the valley, with its lovely lights, and the homes down there, the restaurants, the art treasures, and the immemoriality of an ancient, timeless city.

I picked myself up, painfully, and looked down over the mountainside. Red streaked into the night sky, and I screamed, knowing she was in there, in the burning wreckage. "But she's Gianni's mother," I was screaming, and was still screaming when a car shrilled to a stop, and a shocked motorist climbed out from behind the wheel.

"It's a friend of mine," I said, sobbing. "Can't you help, won't you help? You must help her, you must help…"

• • •

Sirens sounded, in the night, and there was pandemonium.

I knew I could never tell my mother and father about it. It had happened to me, not to them, and I was a grown woman who, adult, had to take what happened to me in stride. My childhood days were over. My life, as a mature human being, had begun. A veil had been drawn, between me and my girlhood, forever. There was no going back: there was only the forward thrust of my life, now and for the rest of my days.

Chapter Sixteen

There was never any proof of anything. Two women had died, women whose days were, in any event, numbered. Women who had lived long lives, who were, at the end, ready—perhaps—to die. I was too young to be positive of anyone being ready to die. But they had lived many decades, had had, for a good many years, the best of all possible worlds, in the fragrant Eden that was the Villa Paradiso. So many others spent miserable, mean days in tenement and slum, without golden memories or beauty to fill their eyes. And died, untimely, in squalor and sadness.

Mercedes and Elizabeth had, at least—until that final, shocking moment—been engirdled by loveliness, each day secure in the golden eye of a sublime enchantment. I couldn't feel deeply sorry for them, not for long. They had had a good life, those two women.

It was the Principessa I thought about in the dark nights, when sleep came hard. She had died, at aged sixty-one, protecting those she loved. She had tried to kill me, but I tended to forgive that, because I thought highly of love and fealty and commitment to honor. I sometimes wondered if I too would not be capable of deeming another person expendable, if that person threatened those dear to me. I wonder about it, and have no answer.

But the dead, who lie in the ground, are fortunate, at that. Better than a living death, such as the Principe. Bereft, querulous, he suffered a mental breakdown. His constant question: "Where is my wife? Won't you please tell her I'm waiting for her?"

The rest of us look at each other, unable to answer. Gianni takes my hand and says, "*Cara*, don't look like that. He doesn't know what he's saying, he's in another world."

But tawny-haired Eleanora goes to him, sits on his knee, her eyes turned inwards. They have secrets together, perhaps. They share something, possibly something horrible. I wonder if they are both guilty, or if one shares the other's guilt. Children are never children for long. The child and the old man, quiet, sit in the sun, their hands interlaced. And a cool breeze lifts the little girl's hair, making it a shimmering haze, like molten gold.

I don't feel anything more for my new family than I did when I met them. But I deeply love Gianni, my husband. Peter said to me, "Barbara, this isn't your world. Won't you come home? With me?"

I thought it over carefully, very carefully. Peter was like someone I had known all my life, the boys I had gone to proms with, had dated, had thought I would marry. But I guess I inherit a trait of my great-aunt's, the late Contessa. I have a rage to live. To see *different* things, to move onward and outward, to discard the familiar and the safe. So I said no to Peter and yes to Gianni. One day, when my dotty father-in-law dies, I will be a Principessa, but it doesn't mean anything; only vulgarians use titles. I will live my life a simple woman, Signora Monteverdi. My concern is Gianni, the child I will bring to life before next summer, and the integrity of our lives, just the three of us.

But I love the villa! Oh, how I love it…every branch and bush has meaning for me, every blade of grass. The late Contessa loved it so much that she never went back to the land of her birth. I've made a trip, to see my parents, but Mercedes never even touched foot on her native soil again. She loved Italy with a passion, adored Florence and the villa just up the hill, with all her heart and soul. And she was fond of its one-time owners, the Monteverdis. She thought they were wonderful people.

And some of them are.

But like the rest of humanity, some of them aren't.

Her will, written in Italian—because in her heart of hearts Mercedes had become Italian—was shown to me by the signores Predelli and Pineider. It was like a poem. I have never forgotten those words from a woman I never saw, never smiled at, never touched. But who, God knows, changed the entire course of my life.

This was her dictum, transcribed only a year before her death:

> *A quell' antico lignaggio di nobile i Monteverdi di Firenze, trasmetto il loro diritto di primogenitura...affinché possano amare la loro come io l'ho amata, e che possano sopra vivere per altri mille anni...*

"Could you translate for me?" I asked signore Predelli, and, nodding, he did as I asked. "It reads, in English, like this," he said, and I listened, wishing I could have heard the sound of my aunt's voice reading it And knowing that it was a forlorn longing. But I love the words she had said, and I will never, ever forget them.

> *To that long line of noble Italians, the Monteverdis of Florence, I bequeath their lost birthright. May they love their land as I have loved it. May they endure for another thousand years.*

I like to think that Mercedes knows I live there now. That it would please her. And that she is aware that a girl from America breathes the soft Florentine air, loves it passionately, and breeds children, as she could not, who will "love the land" as she loved it, and whose progeny, carrying on the Monteverdi line, might endure for another thousand years.

A Sneak Peek from Crimson Romance
(From *The Count of Monte Cristo: The Wild and Wanton Edition, Volume 1* by Monica Corwin and Alexandre Dumas)

On the 24th of February, 1815, the look-out at Notre-Dame de la Garde signaled the three-master, the *Pharaon* from Smyrna, Trieste, and Naples.

As usual, a pilot put off immediately, and rounding the Chateau d'If, got on board the vessel between Cape Morgion and Rion Island.

Immediately, and according to custom, the ramparts of Fort Saint-Jean were covered with spectators; it is always an event at Marseilles for a ship to come into port, especially when this ship, like the *Pharaon*, has been built, rigged, and laden at the old Phocee docks, and belongs to an owner of the city.

The ship drew on and had safely passed the strait and approached the harbor under topsails, jib, and spanker, but so slowly and sedately that the idlers, with that instinct which is the forerunner of evil, asked one another what misfortune could have happened on board. However, those experienced in navigation saw plainly that if any accident had occurred, it was not to the vessel herself, for the pilot, who was steering the *Pharaon* towards the narrow entrance of the inner port, was a young man, who, with activity and vigilant eye, watched every motion of the ship, and repeated each direction of the pilot.

The vague disquietude which prevailed among the spectators had so much affected one of the crowd that he did not await the arrival of the vessel in harbor, but jumping into a small skiff, desired to be pulled alongside the *Pharaon*, which he reached as she rounded into La Reserve basin.

When the young man on board saw this person approach, he left his station by the pilot, and, hat in hand, leaned over the ship's bulwarks.

He was a fine, tall, slim young fellow of eighteen or twenty, with black eyes, and hair as dark as a raven's wing; and his whole appearance bespoke that calmness and resolution peculiar to men accustomed from their cradle to contend with danger.

"Ah, is it you, Dantes?" cried the man in the skiff. "What's the matter? And why have you such an air of sadness aboard?"

"A great misfortune, M. Morrel," replied the young man,—"a great misfortune, for me especially! Off Civita Vecchia we lost our brave Captain Leclere."

"And the cargo?" inquired the owner, eagerly.

"Is all safe, M. Morrel; and I think you will be satisfied on that head. But poor Captain Leclere—"

"What happened to him?" asked the owner, with an air of considerable resignation. "What happened to the worthy captain?"

"He died."

"Fell into the sea?"

"No, sir, he died of brain-fever in dreadful agony." Then turning to the crew, he said, "Bear a hand there, to take in sail!"

All hands obeyed, and at once the eight or ten seamen who composed the crew, sprang to their respective stations. The young sailor gave a look to see that his orders were promptly and accurately obeyed, and then turned again to the owner.

"And how did this misfortune occur?" inquired the latter, resuming the interrupted conversation.

"Alas, sir, in the most unexpected manner. After a long talk with the harbor-master, Captain Leclere left Naples greatly disturbed in the mind. In twenty-four hours he was attacked by a fever, and died three days afterwards. We performed the usual burial service, and he is at his rest, sewn up in his hammock with a thirty-six pound shot at his head and his heels, off El Giglio

Island. We bring to his widow his sword and cross of honor. It was worthwhile, truly," added the young man with a melancholy smile, "to make war against the English for ten years, and to die in his bed at last, like everybody else."

"Why, you see, Edmond," replied the owner, who appeared more comforted at every moment, "we are all mortal, and the old must make way for the young. If not, why, there would be no promotion; and since you assure me that the cargo—"

"Is all safe and sound, M. Morrel, take my word for it; and I advise you not to take 25,000 francs for the profits of the voyage."

Then, as they were just passing the Round Tower, the young man shouted: "Stand by there to lower the topsails and jib; brail up the spanker!"

The order was executed as promptly as it would have been on board a man-of-war.

"Let go—and clue up!" At this last command all the sails were lowered, and the vessel moved almost imperceptibly onwards.

"Now, if you will come on board, M. Morrel," said Dantes, observing the owner's impatience, "here is your supercargo, M. Danglars, coming out of his cabin, who will furnish you with every particular. As for me, I must look after the anchoring, and dress the ship in mourning."

The owner did not wait for a second invitation. He seized a rope which Dantes flung to him, and with an activity that would have done credit to a sailor, climbed up the side of the ship, while the young man, going to his task, left the conversation to Danglars, who now came towards the owner. He was a man of twenty-five or twenty-six years of age, of unprepossessing countenance, obsequious to his superiors, insolent to his subordinates; and this, in addition to his position as responsible agent on board, which is always obnoxious to the sailors, made him as much disliked by the crew as Edmond Dantes was beloved by them.

"Well, M. Morrel," said Danglars, "you have heard of the misfortune that has befallen us?"

"Yes—yes: poor Captain Leclere! He was a brave and an honest man."

"And a first-rate seaman, one who had seen long and honorable service, as became a man charged with the interests of a house so important as that of Morrel & Son," replied Danglars.

"But," replied the owner, glancing after Dantes, who was watching the anchoring of his vessel, "it seems to me that a sailor needs not be so old as you say, Danglars, to understand his business, for our friend Edmond seems to understand it thoroughly, and not to require instruction from any one."

"Yes," said Danglars, darting at Edmond a look gleaming with hate. "Yes, he is young, and youth is invariably self-confident. Scarcely was the captain's breath out of his body when he assumed the command without consulting any one, and he caused us to lose a day and a half at the Island of Elba, instead of making for Marseilles direct."

"As to taking command of the vessel," replied Morrel, "that was his duty as captain's mate; as to losing a day and a half off the Island of Elba, he was wrong, unless the vessel needed repairs."

"The vessel was in as good condition as I am, and as, I hope you are, M. Morrel, and this day and a half was lost from pure whim, for the pleasure of going ashore, and nothing else."

"Dantes," said the ship-owner, turning towards the young man, "come this way!"

"In a moment, sir," answered Dantes, "and I'm with you." Then calling to the crew, he said—"Let go!"

The anchor was instantly dropped, and the chain ran rattling through the port-hole. Dantes continued at his post in spite of the presence of the pilot, until this maneuver was completed, and then he added, "Half-mast the colors, and square the yards!"

"You see," said Danglars, "he fancies himself captain already, upon my word."

"And so, in fact, he is," said the owner.

"Except your signature and your partner's, M. Morrel."

"And why should he not have this?" asked the owner; "he is young, it is true, but he seems to me a thorough seaman, and of full experience."

A cloud passed over Danglars' brow. "Your pardon, M. Morrel," said Dantes, approaching, "the vessel now rides at anchor, and I am at your service. You hailed me, I think?"

Danglars retreated a step or two. "I wished to inquire why you stopped at the Island of Elba?"

"I do not know, sir; it was to fulfill the last instructions of Captain Leclere, who, when dying, gave me a packet for Marshal Bertrand."

"Then did you see him, Edmond?"

"Who?"

"The marshal."

"Yes."

Morrel looked around him, and then, drawing Dantes on one side, he said suddenly—"And how is the emperor?"

"Very well, as far as I could judge from the sight of him."

"You saw the emperor, then?"

"He entered the marshal's apartment while I was there."

"And you spoke to him?"

"Why, it was he who spoke to me, sir," said Dantes, with a smile.

"And what did he say to you?"

"Asked me questions about the vessel, the time she left Marseilles, the course she had taken, and what her cargo was. I believe, if she had not been laden, and I had been her master, he would have bought her. But I told him I was only mate, and that she belonged to the firm of Morrel & Son. 'Ah, yes,' he said, 'I know them. The Morrels have been ship-owners from father to son; and there was a Morrel who served in the same regiment with me when I was in garrison at Valence.'"

"Pardieu, and that is true!" cried the owner, greatly delighted. "And that was Policar Morrel, my uncle, who was afterwards a captain. Dantes, you must tell my uncle that the emperor remembered him, and you will see it will bring tears into the old soldier's eyes. Come, come," continued he, patting Edmond's shoulder kindly, "you did very right, Dantes, to follow Captain Leclere's instructions, and touch at Elba, although if it were known that you had conveyed a packet to the marshal, and had conversed with the emperor, it might bring you into trouble."

"How could that bring me into trouble, sir?" asked Dantes; "for I did not even know of what I was the bearer; and the emperor merely made such inquiries as he would of the first comer. But, pardon me; here are the health officers and the customs inspectors coming alongside." And the young man went to the gangway. As he departed, Danglars approached, and said, —

"Well, it appears that he has given you satisfactory reasons for his landing at Porto-Ferrajo?"

"Yes, most satisfactory, my dear Danglars."

"Well, so much the better," said the supercargo; "for it is not pleasant to think that a comrade has not done his duty."

"Dantes has done his," replied the owner, "and that is not saying much. It was Captain Leclere who gave orders for this delay."

"Talking of Captain Leclere, has not Dantes given you a letter from him?"

"To me?—no—was there one?"

"I believe that, besides the packet, Captain Leclere confided a letter to his care."

"Of what packet are you speaking, Danglars?"

"Why, that which Dantes left at Porto-Ferrajo."

"How do you know he had a packet to leave at Porto-Ferrajo?"

Danglars turned very red.

"I was passing close to the door of the captain's cabin, which was half open, and I saw him give the packet and letter to Dantes."

"He did not speak to me of it," replied the ship-owner; "but if there be any letter he will give it to me."

Danglars reflected for a moment. "Then, M. Morrel, I beg of you," said he, "not to say a word to Dantes on the subject. I may have been mistaken."

At this moment the young man returned; Danglars withdrew.

"Well, my dear Dantes, are you now free?" inquired the owner.

"Yes, sir."

"You have not been long detained."

"No. I gave the custom-house officers a copy of our bill of lading; and as to the other papers, they sent a man off with the pilot, to whom I gave them."

"Then you have nothing more to do here?"

"No—everything is all right now."

"Then you can come and dine with me?"

"I really must ask you to excuse me, M. Morrel. My first visit is due to my father; though I am not the less grateful for the honor you have done me."

"Right, Dantes, quite right. I always knew you were a good son."

"And," inquired Dantes, with some hesitation, "do you know how my father is?"

"Well, I believe, my dear Edmond, though I have not seen him lately."

"Yes, he likes to keep himself shut up in his little room."

"That proves, at least, that he has wanted for nothing during your absence."

Dantes smiled. "My father is proud, sir, and if he had not a meal left, I doubt if he would have asked anything from anyone, except from Heaven."

"Well, then, after this first visit has been made we shall count on you."

"I must again excuse myself, M. Morrel, for after this first visit has been paid I have another which I am most anxious to pay."

"True, Dantes, I forgot that there was at the Catalans someone who expects you no less impatiently than your father—the lovely Mercedes."

Dantes blushed.

"Ah, ha," said the ship-owner, "I am not in the least surprised, for she has been to me three times, inquiring if there were any news of the *Pharaon*. Peste, Edmond, you have a very handsome mistress!"

"She is not my mistress," replied the young sailor, gravely; "she is my betrothed."

"Sometimes one and the same thing," said Morrel, with a smile.

"Not with us, sir," replied Dantes.

"Well, well, my dear Edmond," continued the owner, "don't let me detain you. You have managed my affairs so well that I ought to allow you all the time you require for your own. Do you want any money?"

"No, sir; I have all my pay to take—nearly three months' wages."

"You are a careful fellow, Edmond."

"Say I have a poor father, sir."

"Yes, yes, I know how good a son you are, so now hasten away to see your father. I have a son too, and I should be very wroth with those who detained him from me after a three months' voyage."

"Then I have your leave, sir?"

"Yes, if you have nothing more to say to me."

"Nothing."

"Captain Leclere did not, before he died, give you a letter for me?"

"He was unable to write, sir. But that reminds me that I must ask your leave of absence for some days."

"To get married?"

"Yes, first, and then to go to Paris."

"Very good; have what time you require, Dantes. It will take quite six weeks to unload the cargo, and we cannot get you ready for sea until three months after that; only be back again in three months, for the *Pharaon*," added the owner, patting the young sailor on the back, "cannot sail without her captain."

"Without her captain!" cried Dantes, his eyes sparkling with animation; "pray mind what you say, for you are touching on the most secret wishes of my heart. Is it really your intention to make me captain of the *Pharaon*?"

"If I were sole owner we'd shake hands on it now, my dear Dantes, and call it settled; but I have a partner, and you know the Italian proverb—*Chi ha compagno ha padrone*—'He who has a partner has a master.' But the thing is at least half done, as you have one out of two votes. Rely on me to procure you the other; I will do my best."

"Ah, M. Morrel," exclaimed the young seaman, with tears in his eyes, and grasping the owner's hand, "M. Morrel, I thank you in the name of my father and of Mercedes."

"That's all right, Edmond. There's a providence that watches over the deserving. Go to your father: go and see Mercedes, and afterwards come to me."

"Shall I row you ashore?"

"No, thank you; I shall remain and look over the accounts with Danglars. Have you been satisfied with him this voyage?"

"That is according to the sense you attach to the question, sir. Do you mean is he a good comrade? No, for I think he never liked me since the day when I was silly enough, after a little quarrel we had, to propose to him to stop for ten minutes at the island of Monte Cristo to settle the dispute—a proposition which I was wrong to suggest, and he quite right to refuse. If you mean as responsible agent when you ask me the question, I believe there is nothing to say against him, and that you will be content with the way in which he has performed his duty."

"But tell me, Dantes, if you had command of the *Pharaon* should you be glad to see Danglars remain?"

"Captain or mate, M. Morrel, I shall always have the greatest respect for those who possess the owners' confidence."

"That's right, that's right, Dantes! I see you are a thoroughly good fellow, and will detain you no longer. Go, for I see how impatient you are."

"Then I have leave?"

"Go, I tell you."

"May I have the use of your skiff?"

"Certainly."

"Then, for the present, M. Morrel, farewell, and a thousand thanks!"

"I hope soon to see you again, my dear Edmond. Good luck to you."

The young sailor jumped into the skiff, and sat down in the stern sheets, with the order that he be put ashore at La Canebiere. The two oarsmen bent to their work, and the little boat glided away as rapidly as possible in the midst of the thousand vessels which choke up the narrow way which leads between the two rows of ships from the mouth of the harbor to the Quai d'Orleans.

The ship-owner, smiling, followed him with his eyes until he saw him spring out on the quay and disappear in the midst of the throng, which from five o'clock in the morning until nine o'clock at night, swarms in the famous street of La Canebiere,—a street of which the modern Phocaeans are so proud that they say with all the gravity in the world, and with that accent which gives so much character to what is said, "If Paris had La Canebiere, Paris would be a second Marseilles." On turning round the owner saw

Danglars behind him, apparently awaiting orders, but in reality also watching the young sailor,—but there was a great difference in the expression of the two men who thus followed the movements of Edmond Dantes.